THE HE
AMERIC

JOHN GRA

an orphan whose parents were murdered by the Corporation, he honed his hatred in the inhuman squalor of the Mojave detention camp. His escape and fugitive adventures forged his brilliant personality into that of the charismatic tactician who just might spark the explosive emotions of the citizen-slaves. . . .

MALCOLM COBB

a small-arms genius with no taste for combat or bloodshed. He forsook his vast privileges as a favored Corporation employee—to become a foot soldier in the war for Freedom.

PAOLO CRUZ

the twelve-year-old former inmate of an experimental psychiatric clinic, a victim of the State's ruthless pursuit of profit. His unusual parapsychic powers give the Whistlers a vital edge.

DANNY KLEIN

a savage Corporation-trained killer, at one time assigned to eliminate John Gray. His mission gave him a good look at the Whistlers—and he became one of Gray's trusted captains.

The Night Whistlers

"*THE NIGHT WHISTLERS* WILL KEEP YOU HYPNOTIZED. IT'S FRIGHTENING FICTION THAT POSES REALISTIC QUESTIONS."
—Bob Ham, author of *Overload*

The *Night* WHISTLERS

PENETRATE

DAN TREVOR

JOVE BOOKS, NEW YORK

PENETRATE

A Jove Book / published by arrangement with
the author

PRINTING HISTORY
Jove edition / January 1992

ISBN: 0-515-10751-4

Jove Books are published by The Berkley Publishing Group,
200 Madison Avenue, New York, New York 10016.
The name "JOVE" and the "J" logo
are trademarks belonging to Jove Publications, Inc.

PRINTED IN THE UNITED STATES OF AMERICA

10   9   8   7   6   5   4   3   2   1

PENETRATE

An Unofficial History of the Twenty-first Century

According to most conspiracy theorists, the death knell of American liberty probably began in 1992. Some argue earlier dates, of course—either the advent of the Federal Reserve System or the graduated income tax—but the general consensus, particularly among camp survivors, points to 1992.

Specifically significant was an alleged meeting of financial, political, and scientific luminaries held on April 15 of that year at the Hanover Institute in Tarrytown. There, amidst groves of white oaks and hollyhocks, the first links of the shackles were forged with what came to be known as the Hampton Resolution.

Named for academician George D. Hampton of the Econ-Wright Foundation, the plan essentially called for the alliance of an international ruling elite, a secret but omnipotent body of multinational corporate and supra-corporate heads. Below them would be the functioning bureaucracies, and below them the "elected officials." It was only justice, they said, that politicians be relegated to little more than cardboard figureheads. After all, they had demonstrated their incompetence for decades. Now, lacking in both resolve and intelligence, the political figures of the time were actively involved in the process of allowing the world to disintegrate to a point of instability, where business would be difficult if not impossible to conduct.

Among justifications for the plan, it was noted that, given the enormity of the interdependent international economies, the national debt of the U.S., and the subsequent precarious economic climate, "the democratic institutions and processes have simply grown obsolete, unworkable millstones hung around the neck of a burgeoning international society, barriers to the inevitability of progress."

The establishment of a new world order takes time and patience and layers of groundwork, and it was not until the bitter recession of 2005, and the subsequent urban revolts, that the full weight of the multinational consortium was finally brought to bear.

Precisely how the Consortium gained control of the political system of the United States and other countries is still a subject of much debate among the underground historians. Some cynics say that politicians have always been for sale; it was simply a matter of the right price; and the Consortium, made up not only of the corporations but also the world's leading banks, essentially had the enormous financial resources of the entire planet at its disposal.

The theories vary. There are those who primarily blame the Japanese, specifically the gargantuan Matsamamoto Trading House, which was said to have started it all with their stock market "Pearl Harbor" one Wednesday on Wall Street.

Still others claim the roots go back to the War on Drugs in the early nineties, a period when law-enforcement agencies were given wide-ranging powers that circumvented constitutional rights in order to rid the nation of this plague. These powers were, of course, expanded exponentially as the opponent showed no signs of defeat, and, ultimately, the Constitution was considered an outdated document, completely inappropriate to the task at hand.

Through all of these events the multinationals indulged in what was considered to be little more than a repeat of the "merger mania" of the eighties, although on a vaster scale. The intricate web of interlocking connections became as complex as a Chinese puzzle, with Japanese sitting on the boards of American companies, Germans on the boards of Japanese companies, Americans running Korean companies, and so on. Ultimately, all corporate activity fell under the control of the Consortium and its one ruling board.

No matter what mechanics were used to create the new world order, there is little doubt among historians that the Consortium was the prime mover, intentionally creating the financial crisis and pulling the plug on targeted cities in order to touch off the rioting.

But no one was more at fault than the American people themselves. For who else, when the cities began to burn with violence, cried out to the power elite: "Protect us! Bring law and order! We don't care what it costs, just protect us!"?

When the middle class cried for help, they had no idea that within five years they too would be filling the camps, side by side with the "criminals."

There has never been basic disagreement among the historians as to what happened after the rioting began and the violence spread to the suburbs and smaller towns. Even the Corporate-owned media admitted that the Los Angeles police and National Guard units may have somewhat overreacted when they gunned down two hundred protesters on Hollywood Boulevard and then shelled the emergency shelter stations in Compton and West Covina.

Indeed, all that is still occasionally debated in the confines of the detention camps is the ultimate death toll. According to network newscasts, there were actually only five thousand casualties in that first summer of 2005, most of them supposedly killed in the street fighting. But eyewitnesses claimed otherwise: That there were five thousand in Watts alone, three or four thousand in the Bronx, and thousands more in other cities across the country. And, say the secret historians, when one considers the numbers who died in the camps, the figure was actually in the hundred of thousands. After all, the revisionists argue, there are five thousand unmarked graves in Mojave alone and at least that many again in Chino and Needles.

This, then, according to the clandestine chronicles, is what happened: Having consolidated their own power, orchestrated the conditions for civil unrest, and then ignited the passions of the people with teams of paid provocateurs, the multinational corporate elite simply took this nation over. And then, with variations on the theme, all industrialized nations. Naturally it was not an overnight process, and naturally there were dissenters. But in the end, as predicted from the start, there was no one and nothing that could not be bought or subverted or destroyed.

Even the most astute and knowledgeable underground historians have been unable to fully chronicle the decade of decline that followed the Great Upheaval. True, there were certain events that no one will forget: the year of the layoffs, when even the most principled unions were brought to their knees to beg for jobs, any jobs; the end of the forty-hour work week; the repealment of the child labor laws; the cancellation of the minimum-wage laws; and the death of the Social Security system.

The long slide to Corporate slavery, the slow erosion of all civil liberties and the popular will to fight back—all that was too subtle a process to understand.

But it seemed that suddenly there was no Bill of Rights; that there was no justice, only law; that road checks and identity cards and permits to travel were the norm; that the sixty-hour work week was a privilege accorded to all; that the mandatory psychological programs were available for our own good; and that as the standard of living gradually declined, life became a living nightmare, with only the Corporate lottery as a substitute for vaguely remembered dreams of freedom.

This was life in the Twenty-first Century.

Prologue

L os Angeles, 2030: Seen from afar, the skyline is not all that different from the way it was in earlier decades. True, the Wilshire corridor is stacked with tall buildings, and there are new forms in the downtown complex: the Mitsubishi Towers, monstrous obelisks in black obsidian; the Bank of Hamburg Center, suggesting a vaguely gothic monolith; the Nippon Plaza with its "Oriental Only" dining room slowly revolving beneath hanging gardens; and, peaking above them all like a needle in the sky, the Trans Global Towers, housing the LAPD and its masters, Trans Global Security Systems, a publicly held corporation.

The most noticeable difference in this city is a silver serpentine arch snaking from downtown to Dodger Stadium and into the Valley and in other directions—to Santa Monica, San Bernardino, and to cities in the south. Yes, at long last, the monorail was constructed. The original underground Metro was abandoned soon after completion, the hierarchy claiming it was earthquake prone, the historians claiming the power elite did not want an underground system of tunnels where people could not be seen, particularly since the subways in New York and other Eastern cities became hotbeds of resistance for a short period.

But to fully grasp the quality of life in this era, to really understand what it is like to live under the Corporate shadow, one ultimately has to step down from the towers and other heights. One has to go to the streets and join the rank and file.

5

Those not lucky enough to inherit executive positions usually live in company housing complexes—which are little more than tenements, depending upon the area. The quality of these establishments vary, generally determined by one's position on the Corporate ladder. All in all, however, they are grim—pitifully small, with thin walls and cheap appliances and furnishings. There are invariably, however, built-in televisions, most of them featuring seventy-two-inch screens and "Sensound." It is mandatory to view them during certain hours.

When not spouting propaganda, television is filled with mindless entertainment programming and endless streams of commercials exhorting the populace to "Buy! Buy! Buy!" For above all, this is a nation of consumers. Almost all products, poorly made and disposable, have built-in obsolescence. New lines are frequently introduced as "better" and "improved," even though the changes are generally useless and cosmetic. Waste disposal has therefore become one of the major problems and industries of this society. A certain amount of one's Corporate wages is expected to be spent on consumer goods. This is monitored by the Internal Revenue Service and used somewhat as a test of loyalty, an indicator of an individual's willingness to contribute to society.

The Corporations take care of their own on other levels as well. Employees are, of course, offered incentive bonuses, although these are eaten quickly by increased taxes. They are also supplied with recreational facilities, health care, and a host of psychiatric programs, including Corporate-sponsored mood drugs. In truth, however, the psychiatric programs are more feared than welcomed, for psychiatry has long given up the twentieth-century pretense that it possessed any kind of workable technology to enlighten individuals. Instead, it baldly admits its purpose to bring about "adjustment"—the control and subjugation of individuals "who don't fit in."

Because this is essentially a postindustrial age and most of the heavy industry has long been shifted abroad to what was once called the Third World, the majority of jobs are basically clerical. There are entire armies of pale-faced word processors, battalions of managers, and legions of attorneys. Entire city blocks are dedicated to data-entry facilities, and on any given night, literally thousands of soft-white monitors can be seen glowing through the soft glass.

There are also, of course, still a few smaller concerns: tawdry bars, gambling dens, cheap hotels, independent though licensed brothels, and the odd shop filled with all the dusty junk that only the poor will buy. And, naturally, there has always been menial labor. Finally there are the elderly and the unemployed, all of whom live in little more than slums.

Although ostensibly anyone may rise through the ranks to an executive position, it is not that simple. As set up, the system invites corruption. Even those who manage to pass the extremely stringent entrance exams and psychiatric tests find it virtually impossible to move up without a final qualifying factor: a sponsor. Unless one is fortunate enough to have friends or relatives in high places, one might as well not even try. If there ever was a classed society, this is it.

In a sense, then, the world of 2030 is almost medieval. The Consortium chief executive officers in all the major once-industrial nations rule their regions with as much authority as any feudal lord, and the hordes of clerks are as tied to their keyboards as any serf was ever tied to the land. What were once mounted knights are now Corporate security officers. What was once the omnipotent church is now the psychiatric establishment.

But lest anyone say there is no hope of salvation from this drudgery and entrapment, there are the national lotteries.

Corporately licensed and managed, the Great American Lottery is virtually a national passion. The multitude of ever-changing games is played with all the intensity and fervor of a life-and-death struggle, drawing more than one hundred million participants twice a week. There are systems of play that are as complex and arcane as any cabalistic theorem, and the selection of numbers has been elevated to a religious experience. Not that anyone ever seems to win. At least not anyone that anyone knows. But at least there is still the dream of complete financial independence and relative freedom.

But if it is an impossible dream that keeps the populace alive, it is a nightmare that keeps them in line. Ever since the Great Upheaval, the Los Angeles Corporate Authority and its enforcement arm, the LAPD (a Corporate division) has kept this city in an iron grip. And although the LAPD motto is still "To Protect and Serve," its master has changed and its methods are as brutal as those of any secret police. It is much the same in all cities, with all enforcement agencies around the world under the authority of Trans Global.

What with little or no legal restraint, suspects are routinely executed on the streets or taken to the interrogation centers and tortured to or past the brink of insanity. Corporate spies are everywhere. Dissent is not tolerated.

And yet, in spite of the apparently feudal structure, it must be remembered that this is a high-tech world, one of laser-enhanced surveillance vehicles, sensitive listening devices, spectral imaging weapons systems, ultrasonic crowd-control instruments, and voice-activated firing mechanisms.

Thus, even if one were inclined to create a little havoc with, for instance, a late twentieth-century assault rifle, the disparity is simply too great. Yes, the Uzi may once have been a formidable weapon, but it is nothing compared to a Panasonic mini-missile rounding the corner to hone in on your pounding heartbeat.

And yet, in spite of the suppression, despite the enormous disparity of firepower, in spite of the odds, there are still a few—literally a handful—who are compelled to resist. This savage world of financial totalitarianism has not subdued them. Rather, if it has taught them anything at all, it is that freedom can only be bought with will and courage and blood.

This is the lesson they are trying to bring to the American people, this and an ancient dream that has always stirred the hearts of men: the dream of freedom.

CHAPTER 1

They came shortly before midnight, three Nissan-Pontiac Marauders and a supercharged black riot van with low-gloss deflector plates. As always, they came from the west, moving in a single column, only occasionally attempting to avoid the potholes. Now and again, a ragged curtain or an ancient blind inched back from a tenement window to reveal a pair of frightened eyes. But other than that there were no other signs of life at all.

As they closed in on the target site, the driver of the leading Marauder doused his lights, then a second and a third vehicle followed suit. . . . So that sixteen-year-old Annie Fumito initially saw only the merest shadow thrown up against the brickwork below.

Annie had still been half-asleep when she first heard the low rumble of the butane-charged Marauders, still faintly dreaming of a seated tabby. Her long black hair fanned the pillow behind her. Her left hand gently stroked the animal's fur. Then by degrees, as the purr grew impossibly loud, she had suddenly found herself whispering: *They're coming again.*

She rose to her elbows when she heard their footsteps on the concrete staircase below, then slipped out of bed at the echo of a fist on the door. But it wasn't until she heard her mother's scream, short but frantic, that she finally understood: *They're coming for us.*

She was still huddled on the cold linoleum when the bedroom door burst open, exploding back to the rotting plaster and knocking a watercolor off the wall. Although she tried

9

not to look, she couldn't entirely escape a glimpse of the thing: like some sort of giant cockroach in black body armor, sleek helmet, face mask down. A Black and Decker flame gun hung loosely from the right hand. Then they must have looked at each other for at least another six seconds before the helmet-muffled voice said: "How about we go find Mommy and Daddy."

He was LAPD—she saw that now. But why was he there, standing in the shattered doorway of her room? And why had her mother screamed? What had they done?

It was the silence that most terrified her next: the deep silence, broken only by footsteps and the hiss of breath behind those face masks. Beyond the entrance hall, three tiny glass horses had been ground into fine dust. Someone had also kicked out the legs of the coffee table, while fragments of dishes lay scattered across the kitchen floor where two more patrolmen stood. Then—and far worse than all of it—her parents: mother kneeling at the feet of a beefy patrolman, father also kneeling, their wrists strapped with plastic cuffs, hair matted in blood.

A fourth patrolman entered the room and lifted his face mask to reveal hollow cheeks and bloodless lips. There was a quick exchange of faintly metallic voices, then the crackle of another disembodied voice over an unseen radio.

One of them said, "That's all." While another said, "Then let's move 'em out." Then although there was no point, Annie suddenly couldn't keep herself from whirling . . . whipping her hair from left to right with one last frantic question: "WHAT HAVE WE DONE?"

The rear of the van reeked of disinfectant and methane. Someone had scratched the words "Highway to Hell" on the stainless-steel seat. Then higher on the panel: "Welcome to your nightmare." There were also traces of what might have been blood on the floorboards and a fistful of hair stuck to the panel.

For the first twenty minutes, Annie's father remained entirely silent, ignoring her mother's questions. He ran a small electronics-supply store under Corporate license, and Annie supposed this all had to do with the business. Then at last, in whispered Japanese, he said: "Behind in taxes, okay? Behind in taxes and maybe Corporation fees."

It was raining when the van drew into the Arrivals' Yard, a thin rain that stank of more disinfectant—probably Sano Flush, which was supposed to smell like pines but really just smelled like ammonia. Seemingly floating in the floodlights above hung a sign that read "WELCOME TO YOUR INTERNAL REVENUE SERVICE." Seemingly superimposed upon the message was the grinning face of an obviously enthusiastic white male in a snappy blue cap and epaulets. Here and there, fixed to the surrounding chainlink, were equally friendly signs in Japanese and Spanish. No one, however, took any notice of them.

Approximately sixty other offenders were slowly shuffling through the yard when the van finally drew to a stop: women in one line, men in another, children in yet another. Some still wore nightgowns and were barefoot, others had managed to grab overcoats and cheap rain gear. Now and again, the silence was broken by garbled commands from loudspeakers or the frantic shrieks of children. But no one seemed to respond to any of the sounds.

"Be brave," Annie's father whispered as they stepped from the van. Then again as a helmeted officer nudged them apart with the muzzle of his flame gun: "Be strong and be brave." As a last parting vision, Annie thought she saw her mother whisper something in her father's ear—an oath, a pledge, something. In response, her father seemed to lift his head slightly to the left and possibly even smile. Then, stumbling under a shove from behind, all Annie saw was the blackened mouth of the Processing Hall.

The Processing Hall smelled of alcohol and wet clothing. Although a seemingly vast place, comprising at least the entire first floor of the center, all Annie saw was the thin strip of linoleum between the fiberboard partitions. Judging from the screams beyond, children were separated according to age: infants to the left, adolescents and teenagers to the right. From somewhere beyond the gray-green door, a fifteen- or sixteen-year-old boy was shouting a stream of obscenities. Then just as suddenly, there was only more silence.

A squat woman in blue trousers and a blue IRS windbreaker appeared from behind the gray-green door. She carried a plastic clipboard in her left hand and a Panasonic electric prod in her right. After a quick glance at Annie, she turned her attention to the helmeted patrolman and said, "So what's the story,

Morrie?" In response, the patrolman simply shrugged. "Don't ask me. I just do the grabbing."

Annie felt the woman's hand on the back of her neck, then felt herself gently shoved forward through those doors. Beyond lay another narrow corridor with a rank of red-brown doors along the left wall. "How about ol' number nine?" The woman sighed.

Beyond the ninth door lay a gray room, like something from an underground dentist's office. There were no chairs, only a stainless-steel table and a washbasin.

"How about we see what you got, honey?" the woman said.

Annie met the woman's gaze, then shook her head.

"Underneath them jeans of yours. Let's see what you got."

Annie shut her eyes, feeling the blood drain from her face, feeling her knees actually tremble. Then very slowly, eyes still shut, she peeled off her clothing. When she was naked, the woman withdrew a pair of rubber gloves. But Annie did not actually begin to cry until she was instructed to bend at the waist and take hold of her ankles.

After the strip-search came the questions in another colorless room without windows. The examiner was a corpulent man with an oddly lopsided grin. He said his name was Laplin, but Annie could call him Joey.

Mostly the questions concerned her father. Did Annie understand what comprised a Section Thirteen violation: a failure to pay estimated income taxes? And if so, why had she failed to report her father's delinquency to her school monitors? Did Annie understand why citizens were required to pay taxes, and why it was the responsibility of others, young or old, to help enforce existing laws? In response, Annie periodically nodded or shook her head but otherwise remained silent until the end. Then she said, "Look, can't you just tell me what's going to happen to us?"

At which point Laplin smiled. "No."

The woman returned, and Annie was led along the corridor to a staircase. As they descended the staircase, she was very conscious of the cold . . . a deep and stale chill like something from an ancient freezer packed with slowly defrosting meat. From somewhere deep among the unpainted bricks came a whiskey voice singing, "Sold my soul to the Corporate store . . . sold my soul on the Corporate floor." As they neared another pair of steel doors, the woman lowered a hand and gently patted Annie's buttocks. When Annie turned and narrowed her gaze, however, the woman merely grinned.

The holding cell might have once been a shower room, with tiled walls and rubber mats on the concrete floor. But strips of the rubber had been torn over time, and the tiles were slipping from the plaster. There were no benches, and the thirty or forty sullen young women were seated slouched on the floor along the far wall. Some were about Annie's age, some as old as eighteen or nineteen. After a moment's hesitation, Annie slipped down between a red-haired girl and a thin brunette in Razamataz sneakers and Gang-banger overalls. The thin brunette seemed enthralled by some vision on the concrete floor. Whatever she saw was alive, for she blurted out a string of instructions: "Go for it! Step around! Door right out. Big door! That's it mo'fuck, freedom jus' a kiss away. Jus' a kiss away."

"Synthcoke," said the red-haired girl as Annie sank down to the tiles. "Don't you love it?" She had a pale, emaciated face, red lips, red nails. Tattooed across her jugular vein: Shelly.

Annie didn't bother answering. She'd seen it before. The Corporate dispensaries liberally handed out Synthcoke and a dozen other designer drugs to everyone over eighteen. For those younger, such as some of her classmates, it was readily available at double the price on the streets. One of her teachers had called it the last remnants of free enterprise.

For three, four minutes no one seemed to know quite what to say. Then without even looking at Annie, the one named Shelly asked, "So what's your grief, baby doll?"

Annie shrugged, shifting her gaze to the tiles.

"Just born in the wrong place at the wrong time, huh?"

"She's a Section A," said a blond girl to Annie's right. "Sure as shit, a Section A."

The red-haired Shelly screwed up her face in what might have been a frown. "What the fuck is a Section A?"

"That's when daddy don't pay no taxes," said another girl from somewhere across the cell, "and the Man comes down on daddy's little ones."

Shelly turned back to Annie, brushing a strand of red hair from her eyes. "So is that the story, baby doll? You a Section A?" Then, obviously catching a glimpse of Annie's tears, she added, "Well, hey, that's no big deal. Section A, that happens all the time. All the frigging time. I mean, shit, you'll probably be out of here in three, four hours. Huh? What do you say, Margo? Baby doll going to be out of here in couple of hours?"

But the blond girl merely shook her head. "I don't think so."

Boarding took place an hour before dawn: Forty listless young women marched across a blackened pavement to an unwashed Greyhound. At one point, shuffling up the dented steps, Annie softly asked the red-haired girl where it was they were going. In response, however, Shelly simply said, "Not now."

The bus was cold and smelled of vomit. Although the windows had been blacked out with spray-paint, there were dozens of tiny scratches, allowing a fragmented vision of the passing landscape. First came a glimpse of the freeway pylons, then more gray concrete and tendrils of graffiti. At one point, without even thinking about it, Annie found herself asking the girl beside her the same question she had asked Shelly: *Where?*

The girl, eighteen or nineteen years old and obviously from the Westside, suddenly burst into tears. "How can I possibly know that? How can I possibly know something like that?"

While from the seat behind, a softer but knowing voice said, "Hell, honey. We're all going to hell."

They traveled through the outskirts for what seemed like hours. The houses grew fewer and fewer, until there were only dry, browned stunted trees and scrub. The only other vehicles on the road were military. Eventually the scrub gave way to cacti, and the heat shimmered off the road in opaque waves.

More hours passed, and Annie gave up staring from the window. The bus was weakly air-conditioned in the plexiglassed booth where the driver and guards were seated, but there was not even a whisper of a breeze in the rear. Now and again, one of the girls moaned or coughed, but otherwise there was only the sound of the engine.

It appeared in waves of the distant desert like a ghostly mirage, receding and approaching, one moment clear, the next dissolving.

The bus had turned off the main highway and headed directly into the desert on a roughly paved and potholed road. First Annie saw what looked like waves of wire reaching up into the pale blue sky. Then the waves became walls, high wire fences, with fingers of what looked like antennae. Next she saw the towers, stark against a limitless sky like some prehistoric relic. While behind the towers stood squat concrete barracks—long, flat, and tin-roofed. Still closer, there lay a fifty-meter strip of dead clean sand.

A number of sheet-metal signs came into view as the bus eased through the chain-link gates and between the ranks of khaki-uniformed guards. There was a notice, in green stamped steel, prohibiting unauthorized entry, and another declaring the encampment to be federal property. There was still another in black sheet metal declaring that all facilities were under the direction of the Cal-State Penal Management and Reform Corp.

But in the end, the only sign that Annie would remember was one that read "MOJAVE CORRECTIONAL FACILITY."

The bus rolled forward to stop at a small square in front of a long brick building with a tiled roof. It was unlike any of the other buildings that stretched out behind it. Just looking at it, Annie knew it was cooler—comfortable, even. The antennae she had noticed earlier shot from its roof into the sky. Communications devices, she guessed.

The pneumatic bus door slid open and the driver's voice came over the intercom for the first time since they had entered the vehicle. "All right, everybody out. Ladies first."

The first thing Annie felt was the heat. As soon as her feet touched the hard sandy ground, dry, burning heat. She felt it first on her face and then in her lungs when she breathed—searing them, she imagined.

She wasn't given time for further impressions, for suddenly guards carrying XR-50 stun guns were among them. A burly man with small, piglike eyes pushed roughly at her shoulder. "Move it! Everyone in line. Come on, move it or lose it!"

And then when they all stood in three ranks facing the brick building, an immaculately uniformed man in black leather boots stepped out through the front door and sauntered toward them.

Stopping about ten feet away, he spread his legs and put his arms behind his back and said, "My name is Warden Hank Tull the Second. My job, among other things, is to welcome you to our humble abode. Your stay here will not, I guarantee, be pleasant. This is the Mojave Correctional Facility for federal detainees. Your new home."

A woman behind Annie let out a high-pitched shriek and there was a commotion of movement. But Annie did not dare turn. She was frozen by a chilling fear and kept her eyes fixed on the red, terrierlike face of the man in front of them and licked her dry lips.

She was thirsty, she realized. Terribly thirsty. And with a heart that seemed to sink down through her chest to her trembling empty stomach, she also realized that it would not be the last time she would be thirsty. Nor the last time she would feel fear in this place.

Mojave.

CHAPTER 2

Among the last things that desert-bound prisoners saw as they passed beyond the edge of the city were the twin black towers of the Trans Global regional headquarters. Black as obsidian, they pierced the yellow-brown layers of smog like blunt needles.

By any standard they were an ominous sight, with the continuous parade of TRU-ships rising and dropping from the rooftop pad like venomous mosquitoes in an endless show of power. Then, too, there were generally lights in the machine-gun nests and almost always silver vans descending to the underground level, where Corporate psychiatrists had given new meaning to the word "interrogate."

Although the Towers housed the main division of the LAPD, virtually everyone knew that they were Corporate to the core. Trans Global, the international security arm of the Corporate Consortium, had long "managed" the LAPD—and the police departments of all cities, for that matter. City governments were meaningless figureheads, and police departments no longer even accounted to them. Trans Global was their senior, their boss.

Which was why the fifteen or so LAPD officers seated in one of the Trans Global briefing rooms were wondering why they had been called there by TG's deputy Second District director, Yoshi Sumoto.

The briefing room was long and low, with acoustical tiles on the ceiling and nine rows of beige plastic chairs. There were windows along the east wall, but the view extended no farther

17

than a nest of radio antennas. Along the opposite wall hung two
Orders of Merit awarded to two members of the 101st Search
and Destroy team and a certificate of honor from the mayor's
office. There was also, of course, a Trans Global seal, the twin
lightning bolts in black plastic.

For a long time after slipping into a seat at the rear of
the room, Detective Phillip Wimple's eyes remained fixed on
that vaguely grotesque seal—hands deep in the pockets of a
shabby gray raincoat, a smokeless cigarette drooping from the
left corner of his mouth, still faintly queasy from a wretched
lunch at the Power Soy stand on Fifth Street. Then by degrees
he shifted his gaze along the gray-green walls and began to
examine the others.

Hans the Hammer, the crewcut German, scowling at nothing while his jaw pumped away at a wad of Buzz, the
amphetamine-loaded chewing gum that had proven so popular among those in high-stressed, long-shift jobs, such as
police work.

The Dooner brothers, Jack and Mike, both built like concrete
bunkers, with the same long dark hair and mean black eyes.
Jack Dooner's feet were on the desk and he leaned back in his
chair, arms behind his head. His brother scowled, tapping his
fingers impatiently on the desk.

Jackie Chen. Chinese. Quiet, with a slim build and expressionless face. He had a reputation for knife work at close
quarters. Right now he was simply staring straight ahead.
God knew what he was seeing. A chilling little fucker, that
one, perhaps the most dangerous of them all.

Wimple scanned the others with calm brown eyes before
finally fixing his gaze on one Johnny "Bugs" Collier—so
named, according to the records, in memory of a twentieth-
century cartoon character, a certain rabbit with razor-sharp
incisors. The name had come after Bugs had bitten the ear
off a recalcitrant suspect, right there in the field.

Nice bunch of fellows, Wimple thought grimly, these ugly
remnants of Chief Inspector Erica Strom's Night Whistler Task
Force. Not that they had proven particularly effective . . .
Which was why Sumoto now held deputy Second District
director, why Strom had spent eight weeks in County General,
and why burial ceremonies had been held for Randy Kruger,
Carl Anderson, Ray Lapone, Butane Dempsey, and half a
dozen others.

Wimple knew most of the others in the room, if not personally, at least by reputation. Slash Custer, Bobby Duel, Washington Dupree, Ruger Haas, who had been relieved of his SWAT Team commander position, Dopey Fell, a stupid smile permanently on his mouth, stoned out of his skull as usual. All pretty much cut from the same cloth. Cops who wouldn't have lasted a day on the force that Wimple had joined thirty years earlier. Renegades, outlaws, men who would be criminals if they weren't wearing uniforms. Licensed, Corporate-approved thugs.

Wimple sighed heavily and lowered his gaze to his scuffed brown shoes—Hush Puppy knock-offs, a petroleum product. Then, following a minute of uneasy silence as footsteps approached from the doorway, he finally lifted his gaze to the circle of white light illuminating the podium where Yoshi Sumoto now stood.

Short, thin, his head oddly flat on top, Sumoto was always nattily dressed. Today he wore wool slacks and a cotton shirt, both of which probably cost more than Wimple's monthly salary.

"A nasty little Nipponese" was how Wimple had always thought of the man, but, by the same token, one had never underestimated him. Sumoto was a consummate politician: Witness the fact that although he had suffered demotion, he still had his head after months of whispering sweet importances into the ear on the bed pillow beside him—the ear belonging to Whistler spy Christy Lake, supposedly a Corporate courtesan. To make matters worse, after her arrest, Lake had been rescued by the Whistlers and was now nowhere to be found.

The men in the room regarded Sumoto with something bordering on indifference. They didn't hold much truck with politically deft bureaucrats who seldom dirtied their hands where the real work was done—in the field.

"We are here today for an important event," Sumoto announced. He paused for a moment, but when there was no reaction except the rhythmic movement of Hans the Hammer's jaws, he cleared his throat and continued. "It is an event which most of you have probably been looking forward to for some time, an event which will be remembered in this city for a long time to come. Yes, that's right. We are here for the reestablishment of this task force and an all-out assault on what is known around here as the Whistlers."

The Dooner brothers gave each other an unreadable look, while Hans lumped his mouth in what might have been a smile.

"As you know, we suffered a few casualties a little while ago. Hard casualties that won't be forgotten. But I'm here to tell you right now that those men did not die for nothing, and that Trans Global does not forget . . . not ever."

Sumoto paused, sweeping his gaze across the assembled in what had obviously been a practiced gesture. Then, finally dropping his eyes to the podium, to what were probably his notes, he said softly, "And now I'd like to take this opportunity to welcome our new executive officer, the individual who will lead you from this point forward."

There were at least four more seconds of uneasy silence while the double doors drew slowly apart and a lean, dark figure moved forward from the gloom. Stepping into the light, first came knee-high black boots, then black spandex tights, black Armscore machine-pistol at the waist, black tunic, until finally . . .

Hans the Hammer popped the Buzz bubble he had been making.

Jack Dooner murmured an epithet.

Someone swallowed loudly.

All as Erica Strom stepped just inside the ring of light and regarded them silently before finally taking a last step forward.

"Yes," she said in that grim, cold voice. "It's not a pretty sight, is it?"

And she moved her head to change the angle so they could all more clearly see the pustulous slash of purple scar that covered an entire side of her face.

"Let's call it a little memento, my little Night Whistlers memento." Then as her green eyes grew unnaturally bright and her mouth twisted up into a grimace, she added, "Or how about let's just call it my little Mr. John Gray memento and leave it at that."

She sauntered a little closer, hands behind her back, her eyes raking them all. "Evening the score, gentlemen," she said. "That's really what it's all about, isn't it? They kick you in the balls, you take out their eye. They cut off your ear, you take home their kneecap. Evening the score. Well, lying in a hospital bed for the last eight and a half has given me a lot of time to ruminate about the score card. Which was why I refused reconstructive surgery, because I don't want anyone here to forget that we're still down a few points."

A couple of men shifted uneasily on their feet, Wimple noticed, but he also saw that the Dooner boys were virtually transfixed, open mouths, hands clenched into fists. Also clearly transfixed were Bobby Duel, Washington Dupree, and Ruger Haas.

"So this is how it's going to be," she said, softly, intently. "The face you see before you will stay this way until the man who did this has been brought in hanging by a meat hook. If it takes five months, then you'll be staring at this face for five months. If it takes a year, then you'll be staring at this face for a year. But that's the bottom line. This face is your face until you get me the Whistlers. Now, is that perfectly clear to each and every one of you?"

Then, finally unable to contain himself, Hans the Hammer banged his huge fist elatedly on the desk. "Ja! Ja!"

For a long time after Strom had finished speaking and the others had departed, Wimple remained seated in that gray-green room . . . eyes once again fixed on the Trans Global seal, another smokeless cigarette drooping from his mouth. For the first five or ten minutes, he attempted to make some sense of his feelings, some sense of the dull horror and obscenity. Then, shutting his eyes while his head fell back to the plaster, he supposed that what he felt did not matter. All that mattered was that Strom was back, and now everyone was going to war.

From the adjoining corridor, he was vaguely conscious of Strom's voice again, this time speaking softly to her personal assistant, a wizened little creature named Norman Feldt. With rounded shoulders and thick glasses covering myopic eyes, Feldt had been a run-of-the-mill clerk. But he had been given newfound status with the appointment as Strom's personal assistant when she had first arrived. During her stay in the hospital, he had been sent back to the pool. It looked as if his status had been reinstated.

There were more voices from the corridor: the unctuous tone of Sumoto, followed by Strom's sharp command: "Oh, hell. I'll talk to the arrogant bastard myself." Yet when those double doors finally eased open again, Wimple found himself gazing at Dobie Bloom.

A tall and somewhat awkward figure in his late thirties, Bloom was one of those distinctly bland individuals who fill the ranks of any large bureaucracy. He was apparently neither bright nor stupid, brave nor cowardly, honest nor dishonest. His loyalties were dictated wholly by what he felt would serve him best over the long haul. Among other talents, he was known to be a fairly reliable source of office gossip and was said to write a mean internal memo. He was also something of a realist, which was why he and Wimple occasionally spoke off the record.

Bloom sank to the molded plastic beside Wimple and withdrew the soy bar he had probably picked from one of the third-floor dispensaries. "I'd sell you some," he said, "but it's the first bite I've had all day."

Wimple regarded the mangled hunk of meal from the corner of his eye. According to rumor on the streets, each Power Bar contained at least 6.2 rat hairs and occasionally fragments of rat feces. It was also said that the stuff was loaded with at least two known carcinogens, but then so was everything else.

"So?" Bloom said after swallowing the first foul mouthful.

"So what?" Wimple replied.

"So what do you think about Strom?"

"In what sense?"

"In the tactical sense."

Wimple replied with an easy shrug. "I say she's determined."

Bloom took another bite of his Power Bar, then slipped it back into the pocket of his tunic. "Determined, huh? Well, I guess that's one word for it."

Wimple met the man's gaze for a moment, trying to fathom what lay behind those limpid eyes, whether Strom had put him up to this or the little bastard was simply working on his own. "All right"—he finally sighed—"what do you want me to say?"

Bloom shifted his gaze to that Trans Global seal on the far wall. "I want you to tell me what you think her chances are. I mean, is she going to get herself a chair on the tenth floor or is she going to get those goons of hers killed?"

"What difference does it make to you?"

"Well, none really. Except that technically she's got me on Task Force roster, and I'm not really in a position to back a loser. Careerwise, if you know what I mean."

"Sure." Wimple sighed. "I think I know what you mean."

"So, how about it? We go face to face with the Whistlers, and what happens? Are we going to look like a bunch of assholes, or are we going to actually get something done?"

Wimple withdrew another smokeless cigarette, took a deep drag, then shook his head. "You're serious, aren't you?"

"Sure I'm serious. I'm up for section chief next spring. Now, the last thing I need is to get myself associated with some dud op. So how about it? You seen the Whistlers work. You seen 'em as close up as any of us. We have a chance or what?"

Wimple removed the smokeless from his mouth and narrowed his eyes for one fast memory of a vision he would never forget so long as he lived and breathed: a fanged shadow thrown up on the brickwork, a glint of steel, a muzzle flash . . . then nothing but that haunting echo of a half-familiar tune from deep within the tenement valley.

"Well, it's kind of like this, Dobie boy," he said at last. "You follow Strom out there against the Whistlers, the last thing you're gonna need to worry about is your service record. Get the point?"

CHAPTER 3

The woman looked at the lanky delivery boy with some
disdain. "Why no Argentinian beef this time?" she asked.
It was the middle of the day, but she wore a diamond choker
around her tanned neck.

Dingo, tall, thin, with a prominent Adam's apple that bobbed
as he spoke and a habit of swaying his head from side to side in
order not to meet anyone's eyes, mumbled a reply: "It's from
the Midwest."

"I know that," she said coldly. "Why?"

"Don't know. Shortages, I guess, ma'am," he said.

"God! You'd think—" But then she re 'zed there was no
point in talking to a half-wit and she waved an elegant hand.
"All right, let me sign."

He pushed the hand-held computer across the kitchen count-
er and watched as she slipped her card through the slot. The
machine beeped once and then thermally printed out a list of
her purchases, which he handed to her. "Thank you, ma'am."

Ignoring him, she turned away, leaving him to depart by the
back door.

Dingo loped along the flagstone path, past the tennis courts,
the immaculate lawns, the swimming pool, the trellised
bougainvillea-shaded patio, the Rolls-Benz in the garage,
and all the other paraphernalia of wealth that he saw on a
daily basis here in what was still called Bel-Air.

His job—delivering gourmet foods to the homes of Corporate executives—brought him here six days a week. Considered
slightly retarded yet extremely diligent, he was a familiar sight

to the residents, who treated him with either pity or impatience, depending upon their dispositions. The pay wasn't much, but he did get some of the leftovers, so to speak: food that had been on the shelf a day too long and was discolored, bruised vegetables, and discontinued items.

He went out the back gate to his three-wheeler, pressed the antitheft alarm in his pocket once to turn off the alarm, and again to unlock the starter button. Clambering clumsily onto the seat, he took off down the narrow service road.

Notwithstanding those opinions regarding his consuming concern over career advancement, Dobie Bloom was actually somewhat less the Corporate man than one would think. Point of fact: Within four hours after his conversation with Wimple, he was en route to meet the seemingly retarded delivery boy known to the Night Whistlers as Dingo. . . .

It was just after seven in the evening when Bloom arrived at the edge of the Beverly Hills municipal gardens where Dingo was waiting. As always, Dingo initially appeared as a distinctly awkward figure, slouched on the seat of his ancient Honda three-wheeler. His lips moved in a silent dialogue with himself. His clothing—a pair of filthy overalls, ragged running shoes, and an old blue cap—only added to the impression that here was one of society's dregs. Here was a likable misfit with a few extra jokers in the deck and a servant's pass to the west. A little repellent, a little annoying, but ultimately harmless.

As Bloom eased his unmarked Nissan-Chevy closer, the lanky boy slowly turned his head and offered a stupid grin. When Bloom had finally cut the engine and showed, however, the grin faded and an unmistakable sense of intelligence suddenly entered the eyes.

It was cool among the perfect rows of tulips that flanked the edge of these gardens. The wind smelled faintly of the steaks that Dingo so obsequiously delivered to the surrounding estates. There were snatches of jazzed-up Mozart from a neighboring home and the easy bubble of laughter from beyond the ivy-laced walls.

"I got ten minutes," Dingo said as Bloom drew closer. "Ten minutes before I got to take a case of filets to the Anderson place."

Bloom nodded, glancing at the refrigerated compartment attached to the rear of the three-wheeler. "Okay, ten minutes."

Still farther beyond the garden walls were sounds of a prowling limousine, probably a party of network executives returning from the East Side with adolescent hookers. Then, without warning, came the unmistakable roar of a supercharged Marauder, probably responding to an intruder call.

"Strom is back," Bloom said when the silence returned. "Looks like a piece of hamburger, but otherwise she's the same."

"What's her mandate?" Dingo asked, his eyes searching the far ends of the garden.

"Pretty much same as before. Except that this time she's doing it with her teeth clenched. She's also got some sort of media plan, but I don't think it amounts to much."

"Who does she have with her?"

"Primates. Primates and baby eaters," Bloom said.

"And where are you?" Dingo asked.

"I'm coordination. I keep the books."

"Does that give us a prediction?"

Bloom shrugged. "Depends upon how you define 'prediction.' I mean, you're talking about a woman who's got half her brain fried, so I don't necessarily think she's going to be the model of logical thought. But as far as it goes, yeah. I'll probably be able to give you a prediction."

"What about Wimple? Where does he sit?"

"I don't know. On the fence, I guess."

"And others?"

"What others?"

"The regulars. The guys on the beat, the ones behind those who punch the keyboards. The guys like you."

Bloom said, "They do what they're told."

As always, Bloom was the first to move, leaving Dingo once more seated astride his Honda three-wheeler, staring at the moon through smog-drenched clouds. Having pulled his cap down over his ears and buttoned his ancient baseball jacket to the neck, he had again resumed his primary persona: the slow-witted delivery boy, living for tips and leftover vegetables.

As he eased his bike along the path and then out into the street, he even tooted the horn a few times and shouted at a cat. But all the time, his eyes were darting back to the rearview mirror and the empty concrete behind.

It was colder along the open road between the lower stretch of Sunset Boulevard and the towers of the West End Checkpoint. Apart from the cleaning crews and a few straggling paralegals, the streets were deserted. Then, rising up very suddenly from out of the gloom: the towers.

There were actually three checkpoints between the West Side and the East, three grim stations where vehicles were examined and passes scrutinized. There were facilities for strip-searches and other things, but Dingo was only rarely subjected to anything more than a cursory glance. While, in response, he always tooted his horn a couple of times and tossed back his head with a lopsided grin . . . and then kept on grinning like a stupid fool until he reached the tenement valley.

The streets were somewhat more alive among the tenements, the lottery houses still filled with menials, the video parlors still filled with Devos. There were also still quite a few rocker boys here and there . . . including a kid named Catwalk, who was also known to the Whistlers.

With his white-blond hair, knee-high LAPD black boots, skin-tight yellow jeans, and flowering, oversized shirt, nineteen-year-old Catwalk Hawkins mingled unnoticeably with the crowd on what they called the Sixth Street Red Zone. Menials mixed with word processors, off-duty military, homeless seeking handouts, black marketeers, Corporate slummers, LAPD plainclothes, and assorted informants—all drawn by the legalized brothels and other relatively unsupervised vices.

Scattered along the block were four or five "Kitty Slick" bars filled with teenage freelancers, homosexual pick-up artists, fifteen-dollar love slaves. There were also drug parlors here, generally black and silent, where memories and pain could be temporarily erased. Then came the gaming halls, where a dumb-grinning menial could lose a month's food tokens in sixteen seconds. All while the Lottery hawkers smiled from the alcoves, whispering prices for illegal computer programs almost certain to improve one's chances of winning.

Catwalk paused in front of a window to casually eye a fifteen-year-old girl kneeling among the mirrors. Bare breasted and bored, she wore lace tights and black spiked heels. Catching his gaze, she gently tapped a whip against the arm of her chair. Then, as an afterthought, she even smiled.

Returning the smile, he slapped the palms of his hands together and slid them apart with a quivering flourish—all in an acceptable greeting among the Rorrers, the Return of Rock and Rollers, as the members of the illegal underground music scene called themselves. She nodded, than offered a classic whore's come-on with a quick lick of her lips. But he merely shook his head.

Glancing past her reflection in the mirror, he studied the street behind him: two faintly green and obviously hungry boys from one of the low-end Rentafuck agencies, two overfed johns who were obviously cops. Then, shifting with a slight jerk, he got a quick glimpse of the sidewalk from ahead: more cops, more losers, more everything. Finally, with a last easy smile for the girl, he continued moving on again.

Twenty yards farther, he slid into the doorway of the Zombie Land computer-game parlor where at least a hundred burned-out tenement residents wavered in the cavernous gloom. Twelve giant-screen videos—"More Real Than Real Life"—shimmered from the concrete walls, while Sensound speakers competed in a mind-bending cacophony of sound, color, and motion.

After nodding to a bouncer in fake leather pants and jacket, Catwalk snaked quickly through the crowd, past the rest rooms and through a door marked "No Entrance." Beyond the green glazed doors lay a walk-in closet, then a revolving back wall, smeared with Rorrer graffiti and crude obscenities. Catwalk gave it all just a glance, before moving out through a trash-littered alcove and into the rear alley.

Another a quick look left and right, before he walked out into the alley, lifted the manhole cover, and slowly descended a scum-encrusted ladder. After carefully drawing the iron plate back in place above him, he hesitated, peering down into the blackness. Then, taking a deep breath of fetid air, he continued moving down.

When he reached the tunnel, he removed a halogen flashlight from the pocket of his jacket and swept the beam ahead. Then again, with only half-certain steps, he slowly kept moving. There were suggestions of movement at the far end of the tunnel, but nothing obvious. After three hundred yards, he paused again, took another breath of fetid air, and let it out in a low whistle. Then, hesitating another four or five seconds, he let out a second whistle. . . . Until finally, from deep within the wavering darkness ahead, came a distinctly casual baritone: "Got you, mon."

There were train tracks ahead, ancient and rusted, leading to the door of what had once been an electrical shed. As Catwalk drew closer, he was able to discern the vague figure of someone in the doorway. But it wasn't until he saw the smile, white teeth against the deeper blackness of the face, that he knew for certain: Jackie Arbunckle.

The black man emerged with a slight shuffle, a Steyr M-17 dangling from his left hand, a plastic poncho thrown over one shoulder.

Catwalk nodded first, not quite meeting the black man's gaze. "Hey, Jackie. How's it happen?"

The Jamaican responded with another quick flash of teeth, white in shadowed light. But all he said was "You're late."

"Not late. Just careful."

But by this time Arbunckle's grin had definitely faded, and out came a rubber blindfold. Catwalk slipped it over his head, then felt the barrel of that Steyr in the other man's hand. As they moved off slowly into the deeper blackness, there may have been an echo of another distant whistle . . . but then again it may have been only a rush of foul air from above.

For ten minutes they moved through a filthy maze of tunnels, past creaking girders, running water, hissing steam, and clanking machinery. When the blindfold was finally removed, Catwalk found himself at the mouth of some sort of vaulted antechamber, half lit and smelling of ruptured sewage pipes.

"I hate that part," Catwalk mumbled as he slipped through the arched passageway and into the chamber.

But all Arbunckle said in response was "Now, dis time it's da Mon himself who's going to be asking da questions. You track?"

"Sure. The Man."

"So you keep your act clean, okay? You don't give him no opinion. You don't give him no joke. You just tell it like it is. And don't call him by name."

Beyond the chamber lay a secondary passage and a rusting steel door that opened with a humming alarm. Jackie laid the palm of his left against the sheet-metal, and it opened with a pneumatic hiss to reveal a long, low-ceilinged, dimly lit room.

For the first four or five seconds, Catwalk saw nothing beyond the flicker of torchlight. Then by degrees, six dim figures slowly materialized out the gloom. They sat on stools, chairs, and crates, eyes flashing white in the wavering light, voices hushed and unintelligible.

There was the red-haired little Malcolm Cobb, the unsurpassed weapons master, with strangely childlike eyes. Beside Cobb sat a true child, twelve-year-old Paolo Cruz, who, in spite of the brutality endured as an inmate of the Schick-Gerstman Psychiatric Clinic, had managed to escape with his psychic touch still intact. Seated on an orange crate, dead silent and unmoving, was the lean and wiry ex-Corporate assassin Danny Klein, small, Slavic angles to his pale face and raven hair. To Klein's left, dressed as usual in blue jeans and tank top, sat a blue-eyed and blonde young woman named Maggie Sharp— aptly named for talents that included the ability to take out a man's eye at two hundred yards . . . left or right, by request. Finally there was Billy Casey, tall and thin with light brown hair and permanently bowed shoulders who knew as much about radio and microwave communications technology as anyone in North America.

A lot of things went through Catwalk's mind as he shifted his gaze from face to face. He thought about the fact that Paolo Cruz was said to be able to stare into your eyes and fathom your worst fears. He thought about the fact that Maggie Sharp was said to be able to stop her heartbeat whenever she pulled the trigger. He thought about the fact that even his own friends were said to be afraid of Danny Klein.

Then, turning his head slightly to the left and catching the glimpse of a seventh figure that seemingly materialized out of the bricks, he found himself thinking about a certain videogame called "The Prince of Darkness" . . . one of the genuinely terrifying games where the Beast seems to come right out of the screen, right into your eyes, just like John Gray was looking into Catwalk's eyes.

CHAPTER 4

Having ascended to a raised slab of concrete at the darkest end of the chamber, Gray slowly sank to a canvas chair and lit a black-market cigarette. He sat with his head slightly cocked at an angle, the index finger of his left hand pressed against his temple. His fair hair fell untidily over his forehead, and his icy blue eyes seemed fixed on Catwalk's wristwatch (also black market, but cheap). The earlier whispers had died, and the only other movement was the slow tap-tap of Danny Klein's cigarette on his thumbnail.

"So, how are you, Catwalk?" Gray finally asked, but the eyes remained fixed, hard.

"Okay."

"No special problems with your people?"

Catwalk shrugged with an uneasy smile. "No, Band's okay. Music okay."

"Well, that's good."

A cat appeared, a sleek yellow tabby with intensely green eyes. When the animal drew closer to Gray's chair, he idly extended one finger.

"So what are they telling us tonight?" Gray asked, still stroking the tabby, no longer even looking at Catwalk's wristwatch.

Catwalk wished he'd taken a couple of Calm-aids or something to cut the edge of his nerves. "They're saying that Erica Strom is back in the saddle."

A moment's silence, several quick glances among those six seated figures. But no one finally spoke except Gray: "And what do they say she's doing here?"

"She's got her Whistler Task Force again. They also say that she kind of fucked up and that she won't get rid of that flame-gun scar until she's slammed you people."

"How does she expect to do that?"

Catwalk's voice became flat, as if reciting from memory: "Supposedly it's a three-pronged deal. Task Force is the muscle. They go out into the streets and lean on informers and whatever.

"Part two is public relations—get the menials ready and willing to play ball. For that one she's got the Eye Watch people and a few Hollywood flakes.

"The third prong is the informant program, which naturally involves rewards. Hefty ones. Plus relocation and the usual perks."

Again there was a moment of absolute silence, while the inner circle exchanged quick glances. But again, the only one who finally spoke was Gray: "And what does Bloom say about all this?"

Catwalk cocked his head to the left, as if to indicate the streets above. "Bloom says that the only real danger will come from the third prong—the informant program. They'll bumble through the first one like they always do and totally fuck up the television propaganda. But you got to watch them on that informant thing, 'cause there's lots of hungry people out there."

Gray nodded.

There was the sound of a flicking butane lighter, an ancient Zippo. Then, slowly rising to his feet, another black-market cigarette between his lips, Danny Klein said, "He's right. The informant program could be a problem, especially if they play stick and carrot."

"Yeah, but who's out there to inform?" asked the intense little Malcolm Cobb. "I mean, who are we really talking about? Couple of catch-and-carry boys we used for that hit on the armory last month? A couple of drivers or runners?"

"And a dozen other peripherals who know all sorts of little things," said Maggie Sharp.

"Not to mention all my computer links," said Billy Casey. "Which, in turn, brings the exposure to about sixty."

"Seventy if you want to count the guys who run the West End houses," said Klein.

"Which means dat . . ." Arbunckle began, before suddenly breaking off as Gray rose to his feet.

Then again it was very silent while Gray slowly turned to Catwalk and dismissed him with a nod.

It was still very quiet when Gray finally turned to address his inner circle. Danny Klein had eased himself back down on one of the packing crates. Maggie Sharp had laced her hands across her knees and let her head fall back to the bricks. Somewhere from within the network of pipes above, two or three rats scurried softly into the deeper gloom, but only Gray's tabby seemed to notice.

Typically, Gray began on an oblique note. There was a quick reference to his incarceration in one of the internment camps where his parents had died, then another quick reference to a shadowy figure known only as the Old Wolf. As always, however, these biographical remarks were so fragmented, so fleeting, that one was left with only the vaguest impression of Gray's past: a dim vision of a young man wandering though a world turned upside down with Corporate greed, an equally hazy notion of the boy reading Sun Tzu in the high desert mountains. Then, without seemingly any logical transition, he was suddenly talking about the midtwentieth-century Algerian revolt against the French.

By the early 1950s, he said, Algerian resistance to the French had roughly assumed a cellular structure, with interlocking networks linked by cutouts. On the face of it, the structure was reasonably secure, because no one individual knew anything more than the contact name of the link above him. "But as soon as the French began pulling in the couriers and squeezing their balls, the whole system began to collapse. By the end of a month, the French had more or less rolled back the networks all the way to the source."

"So what happened?" asked Maggie softly.

"A lot of people got hurt before it was all over," Gray replied.

Gray moved to the edge of the concrete slab and sank to his haunches to toy with the tabby cat. "Point is," he said, "they can roll us back. It is possible to pick up enough pieces from people out there to track us right back into the tunnels. Not that they'd catch us napping. But it could set us back a long way."

"So what you are suggesting," said Billy Casey, "is we should pull in the links? Tighten security?"

"No," said Klein from the darker corner. "This isn't a lesson in security. This is a lesson in popular support."

Gray nodded. "That's right, popular support. Strom wants to roll back our links into the tunnels, but ultimately there's only one way she can do that. She's got to win the support of the East Side. Now, maybe she can buy it, or maybe she's going to scare them into it. But either way, she's got nothing without the people and she knows it. It's what Algeria was all about. It's what Russia was all about. It's even what this country was all about in the beginning: Will the people stand up for you, or will they just shrug and walk away?"

"According to what the underground is saying," Casey put in softly, "we've already won that battle hands down."

"Billy's right," added Malcolm Cobb. "I mean, just take a look at the East Side walls. They love us out there."

Gray seemed to smile, but possibly only for his cat. "Sure, they love us, but will they fight for us? Will they die for us? Will they fill up bottles of gas for us and stuff 'em with oil-soaked rags?"

He rose to his feet, the cat now in his arms. "Think of it like this," he said. "Those people may not have too much going for them, but at least they're breathing, and they have the semblance of a tolerable existence. At least they're not rotting in some desert stinkhole, watching their kids waste away in the sun. Now, someone like Strom comes along, and how's she going to play it? Well, first she's going to play the soft side: cash rewards, new life, new home. If that doesn't work, she's going to give them a little stick, pull out the electrodes and start asking personal questions. Either way, it's a pretty effective argument. The Night Whistlers, on the other hand, have only one question for them: *You want to be free?*"

They were still seated in the gloom when Gray left them: Klein still smoking in the corner, Maggie Sharp with her hands still laced around her knees . . . Arbunckle, Malcolm Cobb, and Billy Casey still occasionally exchanging glances. There were also still sounds of rats above and the slow drip of water from deeper within the tunnels, but otherwise it was again very quiet.

"He's right," Casey said at last. "This isn't about body counts. This is about revolution."

Sharp nodded and glanced at Klein. But Klein's face remained expressionless.

"So what do we do?" asked Cobb.

"We do what da Mon tells us," replied Arbunckle. "We wait for him to figure it all out, and den we do what he tells us to do . . . same as always, same as from the start."

"Fine, but I still think we got to look at the liabilities here. I still think we'd better make some kind of evaluation of who's out there and how much they can tell Strom. I mean, once she gets her hands on some runner or something, we could be looking at—"

"Listen," Sharp whispered. Then again, as the softly insistent echo of a whistled tune wafted down from the tunnels above: "Listen."

"That's Johnny," Klein said softly. "That's him up there."

"So what the fuck is he doing?" Cobb asked.

"He's talking to the people," Klein replied. "He asking them that question again: *You want to be free?*"

CHAPTER 5

Although Japanese concerns had sold some of their full interest and now held only nineteen percent of Universal-Tokogawa, both the ninth and tenth floors of the black Burbank tower complex reflected Oriental tastes. Among other touches, the wallpaper featured a delicate pattern of chrysanthemums, while the lamp shades were silk. There was a collection of ivory (real ivory) figurines along the alcoves leading from the executive suites and an oblong goldfish pond—which all but ruined Phillip Wimple's left shoe when he accidentally stepped into it.

It had been just ten o'clock in the morning when Wimple arrived as one of three deferential assistants to Miss Strom. Also, there were her ever-present cocker spaniel, along with Norman Feldt, and a Trans Global socio-psychologist by the name of Dr. Rupert Gringrich.

Facing the Strom party across a smoked-glass table, replete with strategically placed bowls of strawberries, were no less than five network representatives: two story editors, two programming directors, and a particularly obnoxious producer named Teddy Dublin. Earlier there had been talk of also bringing in a network equivalent of Gringrich, someone called Dr. Schock. For the moment, however, there were only the five.

It began on an oblique note that Wimple was only able to partially follow. "Okay, we open with the big picture," Dublin had said. "Start with the broad strokes and work in the detail from there." He then went on to talk about three shows he had apparently produced with reasonable success: "Corporate Combat," "Devo Doll," and something called "Screwing for Dollars."

In an obviously practiced aside, one of the story editors, a rail-thin boy in a blue cashmere jumpsuit, whispered: "And that one took a six share on a Sunday prime."

Dublin responded with a quick grin and then idly ran a finger along that portion of hairless chest revealed by the spread of his sweater. "Hey, I had help."

"And you'll have help on this one too," put in Strom. "But we've got to have a basic concept. I mean, that's what we're doing here, isn't it? Concept?"

Dublin began nodding before he spoke, while his grin slowly faded. "Okay, concept. Concept is . . . What? What's our concept, Jackie girl?"

One of the programming directors, a plump woman with a pair of tiny dangling handcuff earrings, replied first: "I think we called it Devo Busters."

"That's right," Teddy said, beaming. "We're calling it Devo Busters. Not that we're talking spin-off from 'Devo Doll.' 'Cause 'Doll' was really just the catalyst, the entrance point, so to speak. Really allowed me to see it from the bottom up, right? Gave me a feel. And, as a matter of fact, I even— and I mean *personally*—interviewed a couple of them in my office—black marketeers, as a matter of fact. But the point is that with Devo Busters we're talking an entirely new vision. Absolutely dead accurate from a street point of view, and powerful as hell."

"So what's it all about?" Strom asked, toying with a strawberry, even thinking about eating it.

"What's it about?" Dublin smiled. Then turning to the boy in cashmere: "Go ahead, Derek. Tell the chief inspector what the hell this is all about."

The boy seemed to shrug before he spoke, as if to say *You don't like this one, we can come up with a dozen more.* All he actually said, however, was "Crack combat force. Full battle gear. At least six of them. Each week addresses a different area of Devo activity. Black marketeering, illegal prostitution, non-Corporate drugs. You name it, and we'll cover it. And just in case anyone misses the point, we intend to put in for an FCC double-X rating that will allow us a body count of at least fifteen dead an hour."

Strom exchanged a quick glance with Gringrich, but his face remained blank. "What about the Whistlers?" she asked.

"Well, that's whole point." Dublin smiled. "Whistlers provide the background menace, the dark presence, so to speak. Each segment, although featuring the front, will actually be Whistler operations. Because after all, they're the one's skimming the cream right off the top of the shit that goes down out there anyway. So the primary thrust of the series, actually—the ongoing suspense—is the week-to-week struggle of our Devo Busters to find out who the hell the Whistlers really are. They do it first by torching the puppets, but each week they draw closer and closer to the puppet masters. Will they find them, or won't they? The suspense builds, keeps the audience coming back, week after week. Absolutely classic stuff."

Strom's gaze shifted back to Gringrich, but her face remained impassive. "Doctor?"

Gringrich pursed his lips for a moment, then slowly nodded. "Conceptually, yes. But is it simple enough? Will the lowest common denominator get it? I think that's the real question. Sure, the menials will lap up the blood, but will they fully grasp the message?"

"Oh, we think we can cover that within the script, Doctor," said the thin boy named Derek. "Just a matter of scripting."

"And what about the reality factor?" Gringrich added. "To put it bluntly, will they buy it?"

One of the story editors, a doe-eyed girl with faintly green hair, started to speak. Dublin, however, cut her off. "Look, how about we give you the rundown on some of the character ideas? Prelim only, but at least it'll give you some idea of what we've got in mind." Then before either Strom or Gringrich could reply, he turned to Derek and snapped his fingers.

"Sure, characters," Derek replied. "The head of the Whistlers is this hulk, Mr. X. Big guy with a scarred face. His right hand is Mario Kelly, a cold-blooded killer who has one leg shorter than the other. Limps everywhere, you know. This leaves some clues. Right, guys?"

He grinned at the two story editors, who nodded in unison and grinned back. "Kelly is like real dumb. Wants to slaughter everyone who stands in his way. Mr. X has to constantly keep him in line. There are others, too. Real lowlifes. Not too bright. In fact, we're following a suggestion made by our own psychs and using makeup to narrow their faces, give them a ratlike kind of appearance. They live in the sewers with the rats, right? So we'll play up the image whenever we can. Real unsavory crew."

Up until this point Wimple had remained entirely unmoving, his eyes fixed on two vidmonitors that kept flashing clips from current shows: something called "Gee Boy," something else about a compassionate Corporate prostitute named Sheila Noe.

Finally, slowly shifting his gaze to Strom, he asked, "And, uh, how you plan on portraying John Gray?"

Derek responded first with a look that said *Who the hell is this guy?*

While the plump woman simply replied, "Well, actually that's a directorial matter."

But by this time Dublin had managed to collect himself, with an almost cool "What's your point, Detective?"

"I think what the detective is getting at," Strom said, "is the reality factor. You see, Detective Wimple probably knows more about the Whistlers than anyone on the force. I'm talking four hard years on-the-street knowledge."

"Well, that's good." Dublin smiled. "That's just great. I mean, we can definitely use that." Then turning to Wimple, still with that winning grin: "So what do you think, Detective? We got a problem here or what?"

Wimple took a slow sip of water and then said, "I really don't think this is my area of expertise, gentlemen."

"Just the same," Strom said softly, "I'd like to know what you think, Detective."

"Of what, ma'am?"

"Of this show. Of the story lines, the portrayal of the Whistlers. I think we'd all like to know what you think."

Wimple took another sip of mineral water while his eyes remained focused on the vidmonitor, on the indistinct image of a Corporate hero called Dandy Man, who looked like a sculptured rump roast.

"Come on, Detective," Dublin put in. "What do *you* think?"

At which point Wimple took a slow, hard breath and said, "I think it's a load of crap. I don't think the public is going to buy it for a moment, not one moment."

Dublin's face flushed, but his voice remained flat, calm. "This is television, Detective. The most powerful medium in the world. The people will believe what we tell them to believe."

Derek Fine said to Strom, almost pleading, "Are you sure you won't have some fruit?"

Strom ignored him.

Dr. Gingrich jumped in. "He is correct. Our tests have shown that noncritical faculties take precedence during television viewing. In addition, we will have subliminal messages running constantly throughout the program, conditioning viewers to hate and despise these Devos."

Wimple stared blandly across the table. "Let me tell you about the Night Whistlers, Mr. Dublin. The Whistlers are not stupid and they're not rats. And the people out there know it—all the way down to the pit of their stomachs."

"All right," Dublin began, "but you could just stop and think a moment—"

Wimple cut him off, his voice tired. "No, sir, I don't have to stop and think about anything. All I got to do is try and protect you from these stupid and rodentlike people. Assuming, of course, that the Whistlers even give a shit about this little show of yours, which I doubt. But assuming they do, then it's my job to protect you. Now, why don't you think about that for a moment?"

CHAPTER 6

When the Internal Revenue Service became privatized in 2005, taking the collection of taxes out of government hands and placing it into Corporate hands, it became exactly what the Corporations promised: an extremely efficient, profit-making business. Some of the profit even ended in government hands—but not much, for many government functions had become privatized over the years, and what was left in terms of activity or power did not amount to much.

However, thrown out the window with inefficiency, went the already laughable Congressional control of an agency that had blatantly violated citizens' rights since its inception early in the twentieth century. By now, in 2030, the IRS had extraordinary police powers, able not only to confiscate all personal property for the Corporate coffers, but also to imprison tax offenders through the use of a standard form, which simply passed through judicial hands for a rubber-stamped signature. It was, without doubt, the most feared and hated agency in the country.

At IRS Inspection Station Number 43 in Van Nuys, dozens of potential offenders in various states of agitation sat on rows of carefully designed, uncomfortable metal chairs, waiting for their numbers to be called. Bright fluorescent lights glared down from the ceiling, reflecting off stark white walls to illuminate every square inch of the waiting room. The electronic entrance doors only opened inward—the sole exit through the offices facing the waiting taxpayers at the far end of the room. What was in those offices and beyond was a mystery, for the windows and double door were made of deeply darkened glass through which no light escaped.

Two burly, uniformed and armed Corporate security guards stood near the entrance doors, as if to dissuade anyone from trying to leave through them, even though it was impossible.

Angus De Stefano was there because he had been unable to raise the money for his quarterly taxes. His small construction company had recently lost a Corporate contract, and his cash flow had suffered. He planned to plead for leniency on the basis of his previous work for the Consortium and his future value to them.

Betty Khatchadourian had also missed her quarterlies, after losing her job as a waitress at the Hilton-Otani Hotel. What she had set aside for taxes had gone for food to keep herself and her three-year-old son alive. She had no idea what to say, except "You can't get blood from a stone." She had been advised against making this statement by her roommate, who was a Corporate word processor, but hadn't yet been able to come up with a better line.

Nam Hyo, who had arrived from Asia as cheap labor two years earlier, had been sent into the streets when the job ended. Taxes had been automatically deducted from his wages, but not enough, due to a computer operator's oversight. He was hoping the IRS would deport him. While Vietnam was poor, there was at least rice. Here he was living on garbage-can leftovers, and having to fight for them with other homeless people.

And then there was Olga Holder. Seventy-six years old, she had lost her husband a month earlier. A hard-working word processor, he had managed to eke out a living for them both. It was only after his death that she learned he had missed two tax payments—for which she was now responsible. White-haired and frail, she twisted her hands together as she sat there. Secretly, she wished for nothing more than death, for she had little to live for. And secretly, as her eyes flicked nervously around this bare, imposing room, she thought she was in the right place for it.

A door between two of the darkened windows opened, and a thin man with a receding hairline entered. He looked at his handheld computer. "Number 24067," he said in a reedy voice, without looking up.

Papers shuffled as people looked at the notices in their hands.

"24067," he repeated impatiently, this time looking up and scanning the crowd.

"Oh," Olga Holder said timidly. "I think that's me." She half rose, peering down at the notice in her hand.

"Well, hurry up then," the clerk said, and he turned his back on the crowd, making his way toward the door.

She shuffled into the aisle and moved tentatively forward, her head twitching from side to side in an oddly birdlike motion. Before she could actually reach the scuffed linoleum aisle, however, another tax offender suddenly rose. He was lean and wiry, clad in an overcoat and blue jeans. She had not previously noted the man. . . . But now she could hardly take her eyes off him.

With an almost imperceptible smile, he put one finger over his lips in the universal gesture for silence and gently took the notice from her trembling, liver-spotted hand.

"I'm Number 24067," he said and turned to face the front.

"But . . ." Olga began, but the events of the day were all too much for her. She began to cry at this unexpected diversion.

"Hey, what's going on?" one of the guards bellowed from the rear of the room.

Ignoring the guard, the wiry figure proceeded toward the clerk, who had now turned to face him.

"Hey you, hold on," the guard said, lumbering with heavy steps down the center aisle, a second guard close on his heels.

His face expressionless, Danny Klein turned to face them both.

The first guard was a big man in his fifties. Perhaps he had once been dangerous in a physical brawl, but his body had gone to seed years earlier. It was all his brown shirt could do to hold in his belly.

It was the other one Klein watched. Tall, lean, in his twenties, with the face of a predator, he moved with some grace, one hand on the machine pistol at his hip.

Klein held his hands out, the notice in one of them. "No problem," he said softly. "It was just a mix-up. I was the one called."

The guard reached him, stopping a foot away. The younger man stood to one side, another foot farther back.

"Would you hurry up," the clerk said petulantly behind Danny.

"Here, let me see." The big man held out his hand.

Everyone in the room was watching the scene, but when they discussed it afterward they said that from that point onward what happened was almost too fast to see.

The man in the overcoat suddenly turned to mercury. First he stepped to one side of the burly guard so that he was directly opposite the man in the rear. And then he seemed to leave the ground and fly through the air, his right leg bending for a second before unleashing a kick that hit the younger guard on the point of the jaw and sent him flying back at least ten feet to fall in an unconscious heap.

But before he landed, the flying man had turned—and here accounts differ. Some say he turned in midair, others that he pivoted around as soon as his feet hit the ground. Regardless of technique, in a millisecond he was facing the older guard, who was still in the process of turning around to see what happened. When he did, a knotted fist struck his Adam's apple at almost the same moment that a roundhouse kick to his side delivered severe kidney damage, and he joined his partner on the floor.

The clerk was slow. He stood there, his mouth open, unable to believe what he was seeing. It was totally out of context, and thus could not really be happening. Then, realizing that it *was* happening, he closed his mouth like a trap and spun around.

He took only one step, before a hand found the back of his neck. It tightened and shook him like a rag.

"As I said, I'm number 24067. Now, why don't we go and take care of business."

The stunned crowd watched silently as the raincoated stranger marched the obviously terrified clerk through the double doors into the rooms behind the dark windows. And then, like bees erupting from a hive, there was a buzz of speculation.

"We should call the police," one worried-looking elderly man said to his neighbor.

"Where from? There's no telephone here, and we can't get back out," the woman beside him said. "You want to go through those doors after that man?"

The elderly man definitely did not want to follow that man anywhere.

But then a tall black man did just that. Rising from among the anonymous crowd, he stepped into the aisle, sauntered to the door, and disappeared through it.

Olga Holder still stood in the aisle, confusion fixed on her face, not knowing where to go or what to do.

Nobody made any move to help the unconscious guards on the floor.

IRS examiner Frank Roller was infamous. As the well-publicized recipient of a Corporate award each year for dedication to his job, even the public knew of him. And those who had experienced his dedication firsthand spread the word of his character attributes: cunning, humorless, totally without compassion or pity.

At this moment, however, Roller was exhibiting emotions few had seen. For a few seconds he had tried indignation, but when the overcoated thing burst into his office and looked at him with those dark, fathomless eyes, his protests had drifted away and he felt only fear.

A burly, thick-necked, black-haired man in his late forties, he had often used physical intimidation in his dealings with the public; but he knew, as surely as he knew who his masters were, that it would take this man very little effort to crush him like a fly. And another quick look into those eyes told him that the man would give as little thought to doing just that.

The man, who still had one hand on the clerk's neck, gave him what seemed an imperceptible push—which sent him tumbling halfway across his desk.

Roller was surreptitiously reaching for the alarm button under his desk when there was a sharp *thwack*.

A twelve-inch razor extended from underneath the man's sleeve. It waved gently in the air about two feet from his face.

"No, that wouldn't be a good idea," said Klein. "Now, stand up."

Roller pushed his chair back and rose, the fear showing on his face now, showing in the enlarged whites of his eyes and his labored breathing.

Almost faster than Roller would have thought possible, the man lifted his hand and brought the ridge of his palm down on the back of the clerk's neck. He sagged, then rolled off the desk to the floor.

The door opened, and Roller felt a fraction of a second of hope, but a tall black man he had never seen before entered.

"Over there," Klein said to Jackie Arbunckle, inclining his head toward the monitor on the side cabinet.

Arbunckle rubbed his hands together and walked toward it. "How much time?" he asked.

Klein glanced at his wristwatch. "Call it four minutes, five at the most."

"Piece of cake den."

Klein shifted his gaze back to Roller. Then, although he actually said nothing, a length of steel wire was suddenly withdrawn from the folds of that raincoat.

"Oh, God, no," Roller moaned. "Oh, come on. I didn't do nothing. It's just my job." He began wringing his hands.

But the gesture only seemed to amuse Klein, leaving his lips in a thin smile as he moved implacably forward.

Seven minutes after the overcoated figure had vanished through the audit-room door, he suddenly appeared again: hands in the folds of his overcoat, eyes shifting from face to face. In response, one or two of the still-seated tax offenders whispered. But no actually spoke.

"You're all free to go home now. Through this door and down the hall. Your audits have been canceled."

Then, pausing for another second to meet Olga Holder's gray eyes, he stepped back through the door and was gone.

The first four LAPD patrolmen arrived six minutes later. The younger guard was just regaining consciousness, mumbling something about a "gray devil." One of patrolmen remained to get the particulars, while the others proceeded through the far door.

It was easy enough to see where the commotion was. About twenty IRS staff were gathered in the doorway of Frank Roller's office, where Roller hung by his ankles from a ceiling duct—his hands tied behind his back, a moist mouth gag around his neck.

The three men attempting to cut him down had so far succeeded in only removing the gag. Roller's face was an apoplectic red, and he gasped for breath. The primary trouble seemed to center around Roller's ankles, for they were bound by wire and the penknife was having little effect.

"Get me down," Roller gasped.

"We're trying, Frank," the district manager said.

"Let me the hell through," the sergeant shouted. But then he stopped when his eyes met the almost comical form of the dangling Frank Roller.

"Oh, Jesus," Roller whimpered. "Oh, Jesus fucking Christ."

"What happened?" the sergeant said, his voice rising almost to a shriek.

"Oh, Jesus," Roller repeated. "They put a torpedo in the computer system to destroy the records."

"Who?" the sergeant asked.

"Who the hell do you think?" the branch manager said, nodding at the computer monitor on the cabinet, where the six-inch letters repeatedly flashed on and off:

"YOU DO KNOW HOW TO WHISTLE, DON'T YOU?"

CHAPTER 7

The Yamamoto-TRW Research and Development plant in Topanga Canyon sat on six acres of dry brown grass and stunted wild oak trees. Surrounded by an electrified fifteen-foot wire fence, which in turn enclosed a ten-foot sound and motion sensor-packed fence, the facility consisted of rows of low white concrete buildings with red roof tiles.

The bulk of research involved what was still simply termed computer-linked weaponry. It was here, for example, that the memory chips for Arafat-Timex shoulder missiles and the Porsche-Polaroid anti-armor missiles systems were originally developed. It was also here that a techno-psych team under Trans Global contract developed prototype sensors for the Honda MOR antiriot car that had swept the judges off their feet in the *Law Enforcement Weekly* tests . . . and ultimately kept Elias George employed.

Elias George, a black inventory clerk, had punched a clock at Yama-T for nearly six years—ever since the Honda MOR began selling abroad. Considering that the job was basically menial, it paid well enough and there were a number of minor benefits: such as a three-day paid vacation and reduced major medical costs in the event of on-the-job injury.

As for his employers, he could take them or leave them. For the most part, they were either Corporate bureaucrats or scientists. The scientists, high on the Corporate ladder in terms of prestige, salary, and benefits, hardly noticed him; the bureaucrats were a pain in the ass but tolerable. Altogether not a bad job.

The last five days, however, had been the most nerve-wracking of his life.

It had started with a surprise visit from a security officer, Willard Mobley. Tall, gray-haired, an excop, Mobley had been painfully polite when he asked for some time to go over George's computerized time sheets with him. The questions had been innocuous enough. "Why did you stay late?" on such-and-such a date, or "Why did you leave early?" Nothing out of the ordinary, except that normally you could set your clock by the security checks each month. This one had been a week early.

Next had come an inventory audit by the head office. Here again, the audits came regularly, but this time the auditors seemed to spend an inordinately lengthy time in his section.

Thereafter, George's sixth sense—a little fluttering in his stomach, a little sweat on the brow—continued to tell him that things were not right. Not that he could put his finger on it exactly, but it was increasingly difficult to concentrate, with a growing sense that something ugly was hovering just out of sight . . . like a black, ugly flying creature.

This, then, was the message that he gave his "Friend" on the fourth night: Something was not right. People were watching. The security cameras were fixed on his ass like buzzards on a corpse.

It was late when George and his Friend finally met—a seemingly casual meeting in a fueling station just west of the Canoga Park Strip. Having eased his battered Hopabout onto the grease-smeared pavement, George had told the mechanic that the electric was on the blink again. "Could be the converter. Could be—hell, anything."

The mechanic, a balding little man in his fifties named Alexis Vermeer, grunted and waved George over to a vacant bay. The garage smelled of burnt rubber, oil, and ozone. The lights lit only a few feet beyond the hood. A dog shifted on a steel chain somewhere beyond the corrugated walls.

"So what's the word?" Vermeer asked softly, peering into the mess of filthy wires that composed the ancient Hopabout's electric powerplant.

"I think they're on to me," George said, fully conscious of the terror edging his own voice.

"So talk to me," Vermeer replied calmly, reaching down into

the engine with a six-twelve wrench manufactured by one of the Power-Bite plants out of Mexico.

George took a deep breath, his eyes fixed on the back of Vermeer's neck . . . on the two-fingered smear of oil and what looked like the start of skin cancer but was probably just more filth. "It's not that easy."

"So make it tough. But talk to me. Tell Uncle what it's all about."

George shifted his gaze to his own filthy hands. Then, following another long pause, he began to speak. When he reached the part about the cameras, Vermeer may have smiled or it may have just been the light on his face. But in either case, all he said was: "Hey, George, listen to me. Paranoia comes with the territory. That's why they call us spies."

Vermeer withdrew a battered plastic flask of scotch—one of the inferior Korean brands, but still real scotch.

"How long have we been doing this?" Vermeer asked softly.

George shook his head, suddenly recalling the first time: the first cold December night when Vermeer had approached from the depths of this garage and asked *How would you feel about helping the Night Whistlers?*

But all George said was, "A long time."

"That's right, a long time. And have I ever steered you wrong?"

George shrugged. "I'm not saying you're steering me wrong. I'm just saying something's going on. Things are happening, not only in my mind, but really happening. They're unusual, not part of the normal procedure."

"Okay, tell you what I'll do: I'll pass the word up the line and see if we can't put out some feelers. Kind of check things out, if you know what I mean. Now, what do you say to that?"

"How are you going to do it?"

Vermeer offered a little smile, definitely a smile. "You know, give a *whistle*?"

George cocked back his head and briefly shut his eyes. Then, after another hard sigh: "Okay, but don't take too long. I don't think there's a whole lot of time left for me."

Vermeer closed the hood, rubbed his hands together, and said more loudly, "Don't see anything wrong, sir. If you're still hearing the noise—which I can't hear now—stop in again and I'll have another look."

• • •

Three days passed, three distinctly warped days wherein George continually caught glimpses of those cameras tracking him across the warehouse floor or down the concrete staircase to the laboratory. It was also through the course of these three days that someone apparently pulled his employment records and fed them into one of the Trans Global computers . . . or so one of the accounting kids told him. Then again, just after eight o'clock on the fourth day, he was almost certain that Willard Mobley was looking at him when he placed a call from the security booth on the third floor catwalk.

Eight-thirty-seven, and still another hour to go. As a kind of mental safe-point, George told himself that he would definitely stop by on his way home for another word with his Friend. Also maybe grab another belt of scotch. Just enough to make him forget that when it all came down to brass tacks, he really was as guilty as hell—skimming chips from the inventory for the Whistlers for six goddamn months.

Not that he wouldn't do it all over again in a minute. . . . But it was kind of hard to feel enthusiastic about an urban revolution when three Trans Global security officers were watching from that concrete catwalk above.

Be cool. That was his first thought. Be cool and admit nothing. But at the same time, how could you stay cool when blood was draining from your face and your stomach was turning to liquid?

In the end, of course, he could not help staring . . . staring as those three figures drew closer, gradually materializing under the fluorescent lights until he was certain that one was a woman. Tall, booted, dressed in black, red mouth, green eyes—she looked almost exactly like the creature that had been hovering around in his mind.

She stopped a foot from where he sat and planted her hands on her hips. "Hello, Mr. George," she said pleasantly. "My name is Chief Inspector Erica Strom, and you are under arrest."

CHAPTER 8

It took them thirty-seven hours of diligent attention to break Elias George. They took him downtown to the basement interrogation rooms in the Trans Global Towers, put him through the usual psych preinterrogation techniques of heat and cold, dark and light, to disorient him, then shot him full of drugs. When that didn't accomplish the desired result, they strapped him to a table and ran enough voltage through the various parts of his body to light up a small town.

After thirty hours of juice and various alternative measures, the psychiatrist in charge, one Dr. Jonathan Koch—only twenty-six years old, but highly thought of in Trans Global executive circles—inspected the "Patient" and suggested to Strom that they lay off for a while. "Could die on us. Has happened before."

But having already noted the arrest on her daily report (with clear indications of more to come), Strom ordered more. Besides, she hadn't actually slept more than four hours in the last forty-eight, and she really didn't want to be kept waiting any longer.

So, responding with an easy shrug, Koch took a bite of his doughnut and returned to the job at hand . . . taking comfort in the fact that he had at least voiced an objection for the video record.

Finally, after thirty-six more hours of this, when George was brought back to consciousness for the twenty-third time, spittle caking his face, eyes seeing nothing, voice only a whimper, he said, "Canoga Park. Fuel station."

Suddenly solicitous, Strom entered his room from the control panels behind the one-way glass and offered him water for the first time since his incarceration. Cradling his head in one arm, she helped him drink it, a drop at a time.

After ten more minutes of this pampering, she got back to business. "Now tell me the name of your immediate contact," she said.

George was still barely conscious, or aware of where he was. All he knew was that the pain had been beyond comprehension—and that he had been there at least a day. And he was still alert enough to realize that it was probably long enough, on a number of levels.

"Alexis Vermeer."

"And that's who you were stealing microchips for?"

Barely a nod, but she got the answer.

"And who does he work for, my dear? Could it be the Night Whistlers, perhaps? Mmm?"

Another acknowledgment.

And so it went. Piece by piece. All of which added up to not much at all. Vermeer had recruited him. George had said something derogatory about the Corporate world when he was having his car serviced there once, and that had led to a drink and, a few days later, another. . . . And later still, that vital little question: *How would like to help the Whistlers?* Beyond that, however, the poor bastard knew nothing. He had never met—never even seen—a Whistler. Had no idea who Vermeer reported to, where the man lived, who he knew.

In the middle of her interrogation, Strom took a break to call Wimple, ordering the man to launch a couple of Task Force members at that Canoga Park fuel station. But by the time she had finished with George, Wimple called back to say: "Gone. Didn't report to work yesterday or today. And besides, the guy in the banks with the name of Vermeer died seven years ago. Home address was incorrect too."

Then, although Strom briefly looked like she would slam the phone against the pale concrete, she actually laid it on the cradle quite gently. She turned toward the bland face of Koch and nodded to the sweating form of George through double panels of plexiglass. "Waste him. Give him one of those fun drugs you've been injecting into him and give him a lot of it."

"You realize that's going to give us another Died Under Questioning?"

"Nobody gives a shit about DUQs."

"I was just thinking of the paperwork," he said mildly.

Strom turned to go. She had done her job. Not that it would earn her any kudos. Small fish like George were not what was being demanded of her. But she stopped in the doorway and turned, her face suddenly brighter. Maybe she could still rescue this from travesty, she thought.

"No," she said to the psychiatrist. "Rescind those orders. Get him into the recovery ward."

"Whatever you say," Koch replied, shrugging again.

"And pump him up so he looks good."

In keeping with her emotional austerity, Strom had instructed the Trans Global decorators to keep her office simple. There was a sleek desk, a telephone, a computer terminal, the chair in which she sat, and two others. The walls were white, bare of adornment. The windows looked out onto the busy city streets. Beyond them, the bleak tenements continually seemed to beckon.

For more than three hours, Strom had remained in this office, attempting to locate some shred of a link that would lead her to Vermeer. According to the National Offender Index (Nat Off) banks, however, the man had never even existed— at least not until about a year before, according to payroll records. The earlier Vermeer, whose identity he'd assumed, had been a nobody. Just a normal, good, tax-paying citizen. There was some cryptic reference to an even earlier Vermeer, a Dutchman, an artist of some kind back in antiquity, but that was too far gone to concern her.

Norman Feldt's voice came over the speaker on her phone. "Wimple and White to see you," he said.

"Send them in."

Wimple wore a threadbare brown jacket, cheap, baggy gray trousers, and the usual scuffed brown shoes. The man with him—shorter, better dressed, in his fifties, with nervous blue eyes—forced a smile when he saw Strom.

"Nice to see you again, Mr. White. Please sit down, gentlemen," she said, gesturing at the two chairs opposite her desk.

"Detective Wimple and the LAPD looking after you well?" she asked him as soon as they sat.

"Yes, fine," White said. "But is there some kind of holdup? I was hoping to be outta here by now."

Strom smiled. "I have good news for you. There's no problem. You're not only going to get the money for turning Elias George in, but we're going to make you a hero. The name Cap White is going to be on every good citizen's lips."

White did not look pleased. He narrowed his eyes at her and said, "What do you mean?"

"In addition to the reward," Strom said cheerfully, if somewhat forced, "we've decided to give you a Good Corporate Citizenship Award. And the presentation will be nationally televised. We've additionally booked you on the Jack Cool national talk show, and there may even be a reception for you at Trans Global headquarters in New York. We are very, very grateful that you came forward."

For a moment, possibly a whole twenty seconds, White's face seemed hopelessly frozen between a silly grin and an agonized grimace. Then, finally letting his head loll to the side: "You have got to be freaking kidding! I mean, Jesus H. Christ! Do you know what this means? What could happen to me?"

Wimple turned his head to look out the window, to run his gaze along that distant line of tenements to the south.

"Look at it this way," Strom said benignly. "If there were more citizens like you, our job would be that much easier, and we want everyone to know that."

But this time White merely whispered it: "Jesus Fucking Christ!" Then, slowly lifting his gaze to Strom: "Look, that wasn't part of the deal. You were going to give me the money and a new identity and get me the hell out of town! I demand that you do that! I demand protection! I demand it!"

"And you will have it. I assure you. The full protective powers of Trans Global will be at your disposal. Nobody will get near you. You will be as safe as you have ever been, perhaps even safer."

"My face! Everyone will see my face. Know who I am. You may as well put out a poster with a photograph of me on it. Yeah! This is the guy who turned Elias George in. Yeah! Wanted: Dead or Alive."

"Mr. White, you will be far away in another country. Europe you wanted, right? Well, first of all, nobody will know where you've gone, and second, there are no Whistlers in Europe. You'll be far beyond their reach."

Rather than console him, the mention of Whistlers sent him cringing back in his chair. "Those people can do anything," he said. "Those people . . . Look, I just tried to do the right thing. I see a co-worker stealing chips, I report it. I deserve better than this."

"And the huge cash reward had nothing to do with it," Strom said, her voice momentarily nasty, her eyes suddenly like agate.

"I made a deal with you," he said.

"And we're keeping it," Strom replied, friendly again. "All we want to do is increase it with awards and the treatment a hero would get." She smiled warmly at him, her voice growing persuasive. "Look, Mr. White, you have my word that your safety will be an absolute top priority with this department. I've got my best men on it. There isn't a crack a mouse could slip through. In the meantime, if there's anything you need, anything at all—a little feminine companionship, perhaps, drugs, whatever you need—just tell the leader of the detail and it will be yours. We're going to see that you're taken care of—in every way."

Strom stood up. White opened his mouth to speak, then closed it. Obviously, even to him, this was beyond his control.

"Thank you very much for coming in," she said.

White rose, as did Wimple. "Nothing more on Vermeer, Detective?" she asked, with a slight emphasis on the title.

"Disappeared. I don't think we'll find him unless there's some kind of accident. It was a completely professional cover. All the way down to the dental records."

"Well, keep trying."

Wimple nodded, turned, and opened the door for White. The informer also looked at Strom again, his mouth briefly opening once more. But all he finally said was "Thanks."

Strom had only just eased back into her chair when the laminate door reopened and Wimple reappeared.

Strom looked at him for at least twenty seconds before asking, "Yes, Detective?"

Wimple jammed his hands into the pockets of his bargain-basement trousers and returned the woman's gaze. Then, finally cocking his head to the side, he said, "You know that you're taking one hell of a risk, don't you?"

Strom pursed her lips in what might have passed for a smile. "Oh, I don't know. I was really quite serious when I said that the full resources of this office will be employed to protect him."

"And you think that will do any good?"

"Maybe."

Wimple tugged on his earlobe. "Well, I've got news for you, ma'am. These people can strike whenever and wherever they want. You know it. They've proven that before."

"It doesn't matter," Strom said coldly. "We need the publicity. Besides, even if you're right—which I don't think you are—we only need to keep him alive until the presentation. After that, I really don't give a damn what happens to him."

Wimple returned the woman's gaze for another six or seven seconds. Then briefly returning his eyes to the wind and that vaguely chilling view of the southside tenements, he moved back out into the corridor . . . although this time leaving the door open behind him.

CHAPTER 9

When the temperature reached 120° in the shade at the Mojave Correctional Facility, as it often did in the summer, even the guards got uncomfortable—and more irritable than usual. Even in the best of times they were uncharitable; in the heat they were unbearable. The most that could be said for exceedingly hot weather was that the guards rotated shifts more often and also grew more lax, as they used any excuse to go to the administration buildings or their own quarters— all of which were air-conditioned, of course.

The prisoners had no such luxuries. When the temperature reached 120°, there was no solace even in the shade. Nor were their quarters air-conditioned, or even graced with fans. The heat just sat, moved only by the occasional somnambulistic motion of a body. When it was that hot, all they could do was sweat and moan and scald their lungs with the furnace-like air. The feeling that encompassed them all was a lethargic heaviness. And usually, on hot days, someone died—from sunstroke, dehydration, or simple apathy.

Annie Fumito had never understood apathy as a disease until now. In fact she had never even thought of it. But it was epidemic here at Mojave. People just gave up. They gave up hope, they gave up fighting or caring, thinking or feeling. They just gave up life.

They gave up and they died. Just like Denise.

She slept in the cot next to Annie, a woman in her fifties who had been at Mojave for seven years. They talked, but Annie just knew her as Denise. She knew nothing about her past, not even why she had been sent here. Once when she had asked, Denise had simply said, "There ain't no past and there ain't no future, there's only Mojave."

Annie had liked her. Unlike some of the women, she never said an angry word, not to anyone. Usually she smiled when she saw Annie, a thin, humorless smile, but still a smile. Of course, now it occurred to Annie that the complaisance, that agreeable facade, had simply been a symptom of the disease of apathy.

Last night Denise had gone to bed, not answered Annie's good night, and never woken up.

When Annie looked over in the morning at the first alarm, wondering why Denise was still lying there, she had suddenly become aware of the open eyes staring up at the roof, eyes like glass.

She told one of the TSs, which is what they called the trustees, and the woman hadn't even blinked but said only, "All right, get a move, on, kid."

That was the second dead inmate she'd seen in two days. The day before, one of the inmates had keeled over in the assembly shed. One minute working, the next lying on the floor. "She's dead," she heard someone say, and then she watched as two inmates were ordered to carry the body out to the crematorium at the back of the camp.

As far as Hell was concerned, Mojave was about as close as it came.

From the moment Annie entered the gates, she knew that she had also entered a bad dream. And nothing that had happened since had changed that belief. From rising at five in the morning, through the thin gruel they called breakfast, the march to the assembly shed, the monotonous assembling of god-knew-what—some kind of metal appendage that attached to another metal appendage made in another shed, and to another made somewhere else to finally make something that could have been an engine part—through the slice of bread and water ration at "lunch," through the afternoon when the heat seemed to become the only real thing, through the march back to the barracks, the meal of some broth and more bread, if you were lucky, through stumbling to the cot, through a haze of exhaustion and lying there smelling dozens of bodies that washed only once a week with a damp rag, to the final release of sleep when the nightmare ended and some kind of real life could begin.

Through all of this there were the guards to contend with. They terrified her: ugly, brutal men and women who had long ago shed their humanity. The most hated of all, she soon discovered, were the trustees. They had willingly, even eagerly, given away some part of themselves and, in return, been rewarded with a position that allowed them certain luxuries and the power of life and death over the other prisoners.

There were two of them in her hut: Bruiser, who had once been named Janet, and Delia. They were lovers, of course, and Bruiser, 5´ 4˝ and built like a barrel, was the one who got on top. Delia was thin and tall, with a beaklike nose and a narrow, mean mouth. Delia didn't speak much, but her glare was worth a thousand profane words. She liked to watch Bruiser beat up the other prisoners. If she killed them in the process, Delia got positively doe-eyed.

Bruiser noticed Annie the moment she arrived, all that well-fed, nubile young flesh. She walked over to her and let her eyes roam that shapely body. Then she reached a hand out and touched Annie's breast, cupping it for a moment and feeling for the nipple. Annie stood there, unable to move. She felt as if she were being hypnotized by a snake. The main thing that saved Annie from the woman's attentions was Delia's jealousy, although Annie still felt her skin crawl whenever she felt Bruiser's eyes linger on her.

The other thing that saved Annie from that and other unpleasantries was the fact that for some reason Marcie took a liking to her.

Marcie had arrived at Mojave twenty years earlier and somehow survived, becoming an institution in the process. There were a handful of other long-term survivors, but Marcie was the only one who still had her faculties intact. Gray-haired, blue-eyed, as tough as old leather, she was maybe forty years old, although it was hard for Annie to tell because the years had certainly left their mark on her face with its sharp, jutting bones. But Marcie was more like a guest than an inmate. She had her own room, a television set in one corner, a radio on a crate beside a real bed. Nobody messed with Marcie, not even the guards or the trustees.

The first thing Annie noticed was that the other inmates talked about her—not to her, unless she spoke first. But after a few days at Mojave, Annie began to piece together the story, gleaning what she could from the others and using her imagination for the rest.

Marcie had arrived young at the camp, still in her late teens. But before that she was already turning tricks. Apparently her professionalism was a point of pride, for her incarceration came about because she wouldn't give some IRS official a freebee.

After coming to the camp and figuring out which way the wind blew, she became the favorite plaything of a few camp officials: the warden, one Henry Arthur Tull, who happened to father the current warden; the captain of the guards, Blackjack Cooper; the paymaster, Clyde Bellows; and a couple more. She pleased them all, approaching her tasks with dedication and vigor, unlike most of the women, who lay there like rags while the men attempted to take their pleasure. This strategic coupling served to protect her from the more aggressive guards and gain her a few of the necessities the others lacked, like the occasional taste of palatable food and an ample supply of water.

What was truly amazing, however, was that while she survived by trading her body, she also managed to gain the respect of her protectors. In fact, they became her champions and spoke well of her to everyone, including each other. She had a certain kind of integrity, and it meant something to them. There were things she wouldn't do, lines she would not cross, and she established these with enough cleverness and strength to make them stick. One area she knew well were the weaknesses of men when it came to women, and she utilized these, though never beyond acceptable limits.

One would have thought that her preferential treatment could have earned her an early death in the dark morning hours from some jealous inmate, but this was never a danger because she shared whatever good fortunes came her way with the others, and a number of times she interceded with the officials on behalf of certain inmates. In fact, the inmates grew to admire Marcie even more than the keepers did.

Over the years, the word grew that Marcie was charmed. People around her died like flies, but Marcie endured. She'd stopped sleeping with the keepers years earlier, but still some guardian angel watched over her. In fact, when a Mrs. Paula Grundy mentioned that one night she had seen a translucent glow, a ball of supernatural energy, following in Marcie's footsteps, this was discussed among her circle with great seriousness, even though everyone knew that Grundy was nuttier than a fruitcake.

Somehow, by the mere act of survival, Marcie's presence encouraged strange speculations like that.

When Annie had been there a week and Marcie spoke to her, she was awed.

"Hey, kid, help me with this, will you?" Marcie was carrying a table, with some difficulty.

It was evening and Annie was exhausted, but the thought of refusing didn't enter her mind. She took one end of the table, and Marcie led the way to her room.

It was small, but there was a bookshelf with real books in it, the TV, the radio, and a bed with some kind of comforter on it. After putting the table down, Annie just stood in the center of the room and looked around and felt the tears come to her eyes. It was like a home, something that was already receding in her memory.

"Nice, isn't it," Marcie said, and she sat on the bed. She patted a spot beside her. "Take a load off, kid."

Annie sat, not knowing what to expect, but all Marcie did was talk, mainly to ask questions about her life before Mojave and what it was like "outside" these days.

They met often after that. Marcie seemed to like her, although Annie had no idea why. Maybe she reminded the woman of some younger version of herself.

Conversations with Marcie became the only bright spot in her life.

It was only after a while she began to realize that Marcie was teaching her, giving lessons in Mojave survival. Every now and then she would slip in a pearl.

Now as she sat on the edge of her bed, staring at the vacant one beside her, contemplating the death of Denise earlier that day, one of them came to mind.

"Stop feeling sorry for yourself," Marcie had once told her harshly when she was crying. "It ain't going to get you nothing or nowhere. It's just a weakness you can't afford. You're here, and there's nothing you can do about it except do your best to survive."

"Why bother?" Annie asked in the throes of misery.

"Because you must!" Marcie said. "Listen to me, kid. Yeah, it's tough here. Yeah, it's your nightmare. But you have to realize one thing: You can't be a body here. Bodies die, bodies feel sorry for themselves, bodies feel pain, hunger, thirst. You can't be a body and survive. You have to be a spirit living in a body. That's the only way you'll make it."

Annie didn't really understand her, this stuff of spirits, but she knew that if she wanted to survive, there was something to what Marcie said. But the question still was, Why?

"Because one day something will happen," Marcie said. "You can't lose sight of that. You can't lose hope. Something will change, something will happen."

"What?" Marcie asked, feeling a rising hope in spite of herself.

Marcie's eyes grew vague, as if gazing at a distant sight. "I don't know. But something is going to happen. I know that." She turned to Annie, took her hand, and smiled. "One day you'll get a sign. Follow it. Know that it's true. It'll get you out of here, lead you to freedom."

Annie believed her. She had no idea why, but she did. And so she waited, watching for a sign.

CHAPTER 10

The television provided the only light, a flickering blue translucence sweeping across the weeping brick walls and vaulted ceiling of the world where Gray and Klein now sat. Now and again, Klein shifted his gaze from the slightly warped image of a dapper Eye Watch anchor named Larry Luce to the dead-still form of Gray. But in response, Gray neither moved nor spoke.

Typically, there was an odd solemnity to Luce's voice, a slight quaver as he said: "And so, tonight we will witness the end of a human life, a life of crime and lawlessness. A life of a man who preyed upon the innocent without a shred of compassion. A man who called himself a revolutionary, but was in fact nothing more than a common thug. . . . A man who called himself a Night Whistler."

A glance, a look that said a great deal . . . but otherwise neither Klein nor Gray spoke.

"According to police," the voice on the box continued, "Elias George had much to say about these criminals before he was sentenced. How they have murdered innocent people, how they have stolen from small and big businesses alike. He talked of the luxury in which they live at the expense of others. And he talked of their plans. It is an ugly picture of an ugly group of Deviants who wish to destroy everything we have all worked for.

"And yet, in spite of admitting his wrongdoing, Elias George remains unrepentant, a man without conscience or honor. A man who has no place in our society, or in our world."

The camera cut to the chair in which George was strapped, high-backed and uncomfortable, plastic restraints around his wrists and ankles and waist. He was seated in a small cubicle, surrounded by three men in long white coats. On a tray beside them were the three syringes with which they would administer the lethal injection. Three different drugs—two backups in case the first did not do the job.

It was true: George did not look repentant. He did not look much of anything, except dull-eyed and lifeless.

Then again, also dull-eyed and seemingly lifeless, Klein shifted his gaze to Gray.

But all Gray finally said was "There's nothing we can do about it, not right now."

The camera cut back to Luce. "And now, ladies and gentlemen, the moment we've been waiting for, the moment of justice."

A thin note of music from one of the Corporate anthems replaced Luce's voice as the camera swung back to George. His arms were bare, and one of the white-coated figures lifted his left wrist while the other grasped his forearm. A metal tourniquet was applied, while a third faceless figure reached for a syringe—third from the left.

Then it happened very quickly—a single practiced motion, while the camera closed in on the stainless-steel point entering the flesh.

Then, slowly, back to the face that briefly retained the dull gaze before suddenly bursting into vibrant life: lips drawing back into a feral snarl, the eyes growing wide and disbelieving. And finally, almost as if still conscious, the shadow of a tiny smile before the collapse, like a rubber mask stretched and then released.

A long silence ensued, at least fifteen seconds, while Klein exchanged another glance with Gray, but this time neither man spoke.

Then as the camera panned across the clean linoleum until the whole wasted form of George came into view, Luce began to speak again. "What George didn't know, and what the Whistlers do not realize, is how many Corporate-minded citizens walk our streets. It was because of one such person who came forward that this criminal and a number of his accomplices were arrested. And, ladies and gentlemen, this brave man with a sense of duty is in our studio audience tonight."

The camera panned the crowd—a mix of Corporate elite, city officials, and seemingly "ordinary" citizens—finally fixing on a man in the front row. "Ladies and gentlemen, Cap White! Take a bow, Cap."

At which point, Gray finally rose to his feet and said, "Turn that fucker off."

While Luce grew positively rhapsodic. "A hero, ladies and gentlemen! A real hero."

And Danny Klein extended a hand to cut the power, while softly whispering, "Dead meat, ladies and gentlemen. Dead meat."

For a long time after Gray had left the chamber, Klein remained sitting, staring at the flickering images now soundless, an unlit cigarette dangling from his lips. He sat with his left knee drawn to his chest, while his head rested on the filthy concrete. Although at first glance he might have appeared to be lost in either grief or remorse, he actually felt what he had always felt in hard moments—nothing.

Danny Klein lived as a child in a lower-middle class, mixed-race ghetto in New York City. Puerto Rican, black and white, each with their own gangs, all fighting to control the turf. Danny, however, was Jewish, and there weren't all that many of those in the poor neighborhood. Consequently, he was forced at an early age to become a one-man army.

When he was nine, Danny was beaten up by a thirteen-year-old Italian, Mario Petrini, a husky youth with a savage disposition. It was a severe beating, one that left Danny bruised for days. But it was the last time anyone ever beat him.

He began first to study a form of karate called Chinese kenpo, then moved over to tae kwon do, tai chi, judo, and a few more esoteric forms of martial arts before he was done. At sixteen, he had second-degree black belts in three disciplines. He also went out of his way to find the now twenty-year-old Mario Petrini and, after a fight that lasted all of fifteen seconds, left him with a broken left arm, shattered right fingers, and a nose that would never set back in its original shape or position.

At eighteen, Danny was winning martial arts tournaments and attracting attention. Which was when Trans Global recruited him.

The man who approached him was named Ernest. Danny never learned more about him than that. Ernest claimed he was a "special recruiter" for Trans Global, the Corporate security arm.

" 'Special' does not mean you will wear a uniform and investigate Deviants. It means 'special,' " Ernest told him in his low, educated voice. They met at a Japanese restaurant at the top of the Mitsubishi Building. There were no prices on the menu, but, judging by the well-dressed, sleek-as-a-cat clientele, it was not only expensive, but exclusive.

Ernie wore a tailored wool suit, something impossible for anyone but the Corporate elite to find, let alone afford. Danny wore blue jeans, a T-shirt, and sneakers, but nobody gave him a second glance. His companion was apparently passport enough.

"What would I have to do?" Danny asked.

"For a number of years, you will receive special training, mainly in Japan, but later in Europe," Ernest said. He opened the menu. "Do you like sushi?"

"And then?" Danny asked.

"Then you will receive special assignments."

"What kind of assignments?"

"Does it matter?" Ernest asked, raising one eyebrow.

"I've never had sushi," Danny said. It had become one of the most expensive foods in New York. Most seafood had to be imported, due to the pollution of the Atlantic coast, and the fish needed for sushi, which had to be almost fresh enough to swim, was flown in daily from Hawaii and South America.

"Please allow me to order," Ernest said. "You may as well get used to it now. You may be eating a lot of fish in Japan."

The three years of training at the Trans Global dojo outside Kyoto was the most arduous Danny had ever had. His black belts counted for nothing there, and with good reason. He knew virtually nothing compared to what he was about to learn.

He was taught the arts of stealth and acrobatics, to kill with swords and flying objects, and even ordinary household items, to kill in ways he never imagined existed. It was the way of the ancient ninja, with all the lethal modern refinements. It was, he soon realized, a course in assassination.

His fourth year was spent at the Trans Global Academy, situated in a forest near Munich. Here his courses were entirely modern. Here he learned about stun guns, laser weapons, sound cannon, and more. He studied communications, terrorist tactics, including how to manufacture explosives, and more conventional military tactics.

Through these years of training, there was also constant Corporate indoctrination. The history books had been somewhat rewritten (he later learned), to show that before the Consortium the world was a savage, unstable place, where millions lacked education, homes, food, and clothing, where outlaw countries created political chaos and the threat of global annihilation was a constant danger. The Consortium had provided the only solution, but its work was unfinished, all of its enemies unvanquished as yet, and constant Corporate vigilance was the only hope for mankind. He and his fellow students were the guardians of that hope.

He was, by the time of his graduation at the age of twenty-two, entirely lethal, programmed to efficiently kill.

Assigned to Trans Global continental headquarters in New York, he worked out of a highly classified outfit called the Special Collections and Repossessions Office, headed up by a Joseph Donnelly, a nasty piece of Irish work in his early fifties. Red-faced, pot-bellied, loud and uncouth, Donnelly was the consummate bureaucrat. His appearance and manner gave no clue of the superb Machiavellian mind that clicked away behind the loud laughter and filthy jokes.

Donnelly, for some reason, liked Danny immediately. "My token Jewboy," he called him good-naturedly. And he soon learned to add "And better than all you fucks put together."

Danny's first assignment was to show a recalcitrant Corporate industrialist the error of his ways. Apparently the man was questioning Corporate policy—publicly. "I want a mess," Donnelly said. "I want a loud message. I want him splattered all over the pavement."

This was, in a literal manner, fairly easy to do. After disposing of the man's two bodyguards, a totally inept excop and a street bruiser, Danny threw the man off the balcony of his Fifth Avenue penthouse suite, making more of a mess than a crate of tomatoes—and considerably louder.

Danny was soon exorbitantly well paid, with his own apartment on Fifth Avenue, a passport that allowed him, unlike most Americans, to go anywhere in the world, his pick of Corporate women, and entree into all but the highest levels of Corporate life.

It was a very different life from the spartan training he had received, or his earlier beginnings in the ghetto, where food was sometimes there and sometimes not and always bland and the women hustled you for nickels and dimes. His father had died while he was in Germany, so he used some of the money to support his mother—not exorbitantly, for she could not have accepted a sudden drastic change of lifestyle, but enough to keep her fed and clothed and comfortable in her last days.

In reality, he spent very little of the money he made on her.

While he worked hard, because of the stresses associated with his activities, he also had a total of about three months a year paid leave, spread between assignments. He used these periods to spread his funds around the world, although his investments were mainly concentrated in South America, an area where Corporate links were not forged as strongly as in the East and industrialized West.

It was his nest egg, his fuck-you money, his escape. For one thing Danny knew after the first year in his job was that he was as dispensable as the men and women he dispensed. He worked for a conscienceless creature, one which did not subscribe to concepts such as trust and loyalty. It was an expedient creature, one that constantly rolled forward, crushing everything in its way. Its momentum was remorseless and automatic.

After five years in the Special Collections and Repossessions Office, the nightmares began. The faces of his victims in their last moments began to haunt him. And his cynicism began to grow. In the beginning he had never questioned his assignments. They had been for the Corporate good, and that was good enough for him. He still didn't question them—not aloud—but he began to study the files of his victims with a new diligence and discovered that not all were criminals and Deviants. A vast number were simply those foolish enough to question the Consortium's methods and goals. And some were merely involved in personal vendettas of one kind or another with Corporate executives.

After seven years, faced with a particularly revolting and petty assignment, Klein simply left, heading for Los Angeles to kill John Gray. Heading out to kill the man, or more likely die trying. But at some point, before anything even started going down, Gray had stepped out of thin air, looked him in the eyes, and said, "Guess what? I've been there too. Now, how about playing on my team for a while?"

•   •   •

Klein rose to his feet and tried to light that cigarette still between his lips. Although he wasn't precisely certain what Larry Luce was saying now, the camera was very definitely panning back to George's body, now laid out beneath a rubber sheet, the bare feet tagged and the left wrist dangling.

"Guess what?" Klein whispered, "I've been there too," and he switched off the screen.

CHAPTER 11

Among others in attendance at the Matsushita-Universal Sheraton to celebrate the regional Outstanding Citizenship Awards were Bo and Sis Armstrong of the Young American Song and Dance Ensemble, Buzz Tosh of the ABC series "Yes, Sir!" and famed pop psychologist and radio host Dr. I. "Lulu" Canastra. Representing the National Association of Colored People for Law and Order was William Shalan Brown, while Dr. Felix Mendoza carried the banner for the National Association of Hispanics for Safe Streets. Then, of course, there were the usual array of state and city officials, including the mayor and former ex-Miss Manila, Joyce Lutice, and the ever-popular director of civil obedience, Major Cash McCloy. But, given what really lay behind the proceedings that night, even Trans Global Continental Chairman Jason Englund took a back seat to Cap White.

Although his tuxedo (in black spandex) may have been a trifle tight in the crotch, Cap White had finally begun to enjoy himself. In addition to the food (blood-red raw tuna, reasonably pollutant-free oysters on a half shell, and farm-grown crab on a bed of crushed ice), he was thoroughly in love with the fifteen-year-old Brazilian girl that Trans Global had provided as his escort.

He also rather liked the sense of power, the fact that he was not only seated just left of Jason Englund and just right of Erica Strom, but that six—count 'em, *six*—fully armed guards in white tuxedos were specifically charged with keeping Cap alive. And if all that weren't enough, they even promised he could keep the gold electroplated fist that constituted his award.

Appropriately, the Gold Fist of Order had been presented by Englund. Then, although White's acceptance speech (written on his behalf by one of Strom's people) had only been two minutes, the applause had been genuine enough. Moreover, there was still to be anticipated the "Members Only" reception at Trans Global New York's Club Two Thousand, where delights, both culinary and otherwise, were said to be beyond the scope of normal human imagination. And all, as Englund had so firmly promised, as a prelude to the luxurious obscurity that only a million-five in Eurodollars could buy.

Englund, White was surprised to discover, once his awe had been dissolved by a glass of Napa wine served in elegant crystal, was actually a nice guy. Short, rotund, and bald, with dark brown eyes and a double chin, Englund was in his early fifties. He dominated the table, full of jokes, and quite charming.

"Well, Mr. White, where is it you're going to spend all this money we're giving you again? Spain? I'll give you the addresses of some very obliging señoritas there. One of my favorite countries and people. Always known how to handle criminals there. Can't be anything wrong with a people that invented the Inquisition, can there?"

White had never heard of the Inquisition, had no idea what he was talking about, but he laughed along with the others.

Television crews still roamed the room, but White had become used to them now, could actually sense when the camera's lens swiveled in his direction and instinctively gave it his profile—always his best feature. Not that he necessarily loved the attention, but by the same token, with every passing hour, Europe looked less and less appealing. Because, after all, what could Spain offer that one couldn't get in the States? . . . Except possibly a stainless steel dart in the spine, courtesy of the Night Whistlers?

Flanked by two of the guards (with two more ahead), Cap White stumbled on the steps as he walked out of the hotel. He had probably had one too many glasses of that Napa stuff, but what the hell, it was his night, and he could do as he pleased.

In fact, when he got back to his hotel he would definitely get one of the more obliging guards to bring up that little Brazilian number, or maybe that Eurasian kid from two nights earlier. Talk about physical contortions.

He hesitated at the base of the steps for one last look at the wavering crowds that thronged opposite ends of the street: menials. Meanwhile his limousine—armored, of course—waited respectfully curbside. He had particularly asked for the pink one; all the others waiting out there were black and gray. Long, sleek machines with dark, projectile-proof windows.

The driver must have seen them approach, for he opened the rear door automatically with the push of a control button. One of his guards got in first, then White, then the other. The other two guards entered the limo behind them. They would follow close behind, as always.

"Back to the Otani," a guard said into the intercom.

The limo moved off, a smooth burst of barely noticeable power wheeling it around the concourse and into the street.

"You guys like a drink?" White asked. He pressed a button on his armrest and the bar slid out toward them.

"Nah," said one of the men. The other yawned, not answering.

As White leaned forward to pour himself a drink, the limo slowed, then stopped at a red light.

The window of the driver's partition slid down.

White looked up questioningly as the driver turned and his face appeared.

It was thin, sharply defined, a thatch of raven hair sticking out from beneath the cap.

It wasn't the face of the regular driver.

And then White no longer saw the face, saw only the small high-compression air pistol rising with the man's hand and heard the two soft plops and swung his head disbelievingly from side to side as his two guards grew suddenly stiff and wide-eyed, neat holes in their foreheads.

"Where to, sir?" Danny Klein asked.

Fear paralyzed White, holding him stiffly in its grasp. The partition window slid shut before he could open his mouth, and the limo took off against the red traffic light with a squeal of tires.

Klein shifted his eyes to the rearview mirror and the reflection of a black limo still stationary at the light. Then, as if suddenly unleashed, it burst on through the intersection amidst another scream of rubber. Good, he had gained about five seconds, which was all he had needed.

He heard the radio come to life with a scramble of slightly frantic voices: "TRU-ship Scoot Nine from Rover Detail Two. TRU-ship Scoot Nine . . . Reading, Rover Detail Two. We have a situation red. I repeat, situation red."

Klein took the first corner hard as another chorus of frantic voices responded from Central Control, and someone began screaming for air cover. But when he glanced back at the mirror, he saw only White's face nearing the color of his name.

Another corner, and then a long straight, while that black limo in pursuit bore down from a hundred yards behind.

Klein punched home the cruise control, reached for the canvas bag on the seat beside him, and withdrew a modified M-100 fragmentation grenade (courtesy of Aerodyne Torrance). He held it in his right hand and took control of the wheel again with his left.

Moving out into the center of the street, he suddenly swung hard to the right into one of narrow side streets where a year of litter lay uncollected along the curb. Then another fast right into the Second Street bypass, and another quick punch at the cruise-control button as his thumb descended to the timer: five seconds.

Then he opened his door and peered ahead toward the open manhole below the Third underpass.

He braked hard, both heels on the rubberized pedal to send his limo skidding one down to fifteen KPHs. Then, glancing back at the rearview mirror and the empty lane behind, he shouldered the door open and leapt.

A twenty-foot roll left him only slightly bruised and no more than four feet from that yawning manhole. Another quick twist and he was in . . . into an absolute darkness that only grew briefly light when Cap White's limo exploded into flame.

Then came the screech of more tires and what sounded like more frantic radio voices. Somebody quite close began shouting "Jesus Fucking Christ!" over and over. While somebody else shouted, "Well, let's at least find the son of a bitch who did it."

But by that time, Klein had already eased the manhole cover into place and dropped into the deeper blackness below.

CHAPTER 12

Jackie Chen and Dopey Fell, both members of the LAPD Whistler Task Force, sauntered through the evening crowds on Western Avenue, their black uniforms cutting through the menials and pleasure-seekers like the bows of a ship. Loiterers flicked their eyes at the two men, then quickly away.

"Cocksucker should be around here somewhere," Fell said. He spat off to his left, missing the sidewalk and landing it on the right foot of a club barker. The man seemed about to say something, then changed his mind. "Come and see the two most beautiful women in the world! Live sex onstage!" he continued.

Chen looked oblivious to it all. Although his eyes scanned the crowd, they hardly seemed to move in the cold, expression-less setting of his face. Slight of build, he seemed even smaller beside the lanky Fell, but he moved with a studied economy that gave a lethal purposefulness to his motions.

Two men arguing in front of a betting station suddenly came to blows. Half a dozen spectators egged them on. Both policemen gave them little more than a bored sidelong glance as they moved along.

A woman wearing a transparent golden dress stepped from a doorway and smiled as they approached. "Hey, Dopey. How's it hanging?"

He drew to a stop and looked at her nipples, perfectly visible through the material. "Looking good, Sally. Looking good. Seen the Yodeler around?"

"The newsman? I saw him in the neighborhood about an hour ago. Heading in that direction," she said, inclining her head down the street.

Fell nodded. "See you 'round."

"Hey." She reached a slim hand out and rubbed the palm on his groin. "Come back for a freebee."

"Yeah," he said.

They walked on. "Got legs like a pair of pliers," Fell explained. "Squeezes the last drop right out of you."

Chen didn't reply.

Two kids shot by on electric skateboards, weaving through the crowds at twenty-five miles an hour.

The cops stopped at a betting booth. The bookie, an elderly black man with a gray beard and closely cropped white hair, continued punching keys on his video console without looking up.

"Seen the Yodeler?" Fell asked.

"Should be at Bennie's," the man replied, barely moving his lips.

They crossed the street, walking a little more briskly now. The neon sign outside Bennie's said "Liquor—Drugs—Best for Less."

About twenty people filled the small bar. A few played large-screen vid games, but most just leaned up against the bar and blankly watched a game show on the overhead television screens.

At the far end of the bar, a small bald man watched them approach through thick spectacles.

"Hi, Yodeler," Fell said slipping, onto the stool beside him. Chen stood a foot away and watched.

"Hi, Dopey. What's new?"

"Well, you should know that. You and that little underground rag that you write for," Fell said.

"Not much." Yodeler's myopic eyes widened. "You got something for me?"

Although the underground newspapers were technically illegal, they were for the most part tolerated—mainly because they would have been impossible to eradicate. The Corporate stranglehold on all major media left a vacuum filled by entrepreneurs. Reporting on local events not covered by the major media and the news behind the news, so to speak, the underground papers were left alone as long as they didn't step over the line to outright dissension with Corporate-think.

"No, you got something for me, Yodeler," Fell said.

The newsman looked at Chen, didn't like what he saw, and looked back at Fell. "What's that, Dopey?"

"Understand you wrote a piece on Whistlers killing Cap White. Wondered how you knew a Whistler drove the limo he was in."

"I don't know what you're talking about. I didn't write a story about that."

Fell's hand whipped out and returned with the Yodeler's glasses. He dropped them to the floor and carefully stomped one large boot on them.

"What you do that for?" the Yodeler said, eyes trying to focus on the policeman.

"Didn't say what I wanted you to say," Fell said. He took a piece of narco-gum from his pocket and popped it into his mouth.

"Look," the Yodeler wheedled, "you know I can't reveal my sources. Nobody would trust me. I'd be without a job."

"Better'n being without a life," Fell said.

"Look, I done nothing wrong," the Yodeler said, his eyes moving to Chen.

Fell slowly stood up. He stared at the man for a moment, then grabbed the lapels of the Yodeler's jacket and lifted him from his stool and shoved him onto the bar.

The other patrons watched, trying to appear as though they were ignoring the whole scene.

"I want a name, you little fuck," Fell said, pushing his face close.

"It was a cop that told me," the Yodeler said. "It was one of you fucking guys, for Chrissakes!"

"Who?"

"He'd fucking kill me! You got to be kidding!"

"Well, we'd like to know who it is, Yodeler. See, how do we know it wasn't one of them Whistlers you talked to?"

"It was a cop!"

Fell glared at him. "The Chinaman here? He's real good with a knife. Tell me the fucking name or he'll kill you now. What would you rather be: dead now or dead later?"

"I don't want to be dead at all," the man whimpered.

"Come on," Fell said, giving him a little tug.

A tear rolled down the Yodeler's cheek.

"Ah, for Chrissakes," Fell said disgustedly. He turned his head to Chen. "Want to cut this one up?"

"It was Chuck Avery, downtown," the Yodeler said. "I was having a goddamn drink with Avery and he told me."

Both cops knew Avery. He'd been a sergeant for twenty years and a drunk for thirty.

"Well, see, that wasn't so bad," Fell said, releasing his lapels.

"Don't tell Avery. Please," the little man said.

Fell smiled and said to his partner, "What you think, Jackie? The little fuck is scared of Avery. Gotta be the only person left in the city scared of Avery."

"I think we should end his misery," Chen said softly.

And then, in a motion too fast to see, a six-inch wide-bladed knife appeared in his hand and slashed upward, sliding neatly between the little writer's ribs and into his heart.

The Yodeler's eyes opened wide and he stared into Chen's face. He started to speak but could only gurgle.

With a deft motion, Chen pulled the knife back out. For a moment the man sat there, frozen in position, then he toppled backward to lie on the bar.

Fell looked at the body, chewed his gum three times, and said matter-of-factly, "What you do that for, Jackie?"

The knife had disappeared. Chen rubbed his right palm with his left thumb. "He irritated me. I don't like whiners," he said.

"I'll keep that in mind," Fell said, and he walked for the door without a backward glance.

Jason Englund leaned back in the chair, held his hands out, and examined his fingernails.

"Very good, Alicia," he said to the pert blonde manicurist kneeling before him. "That'll do for now."

She packed her instruments carefully back into the case and rose. "Is there anything else, Mr. Englund?" she asked, eyes submissively downcast.

"I may need you later," he said.

"Yes, sir."

He watched the movement of her hips as she left the room, then turned his attention to Erica Strom.

She sat in an armchair to his left, her legs crossed, dressed in black as usual.

"A pretty girl, isn't she?" Englund said.

"Yes," Strom replied.

He got up and walked to the oak liquor cabinet. There was a Monet on the wall, a Persian carpet on the floor, a tall Degas sculpture in one corner. Although this mansion in the Bel Air hills was only his West Coast home, it was furnished for a king. She had seen his New York brownstone, however, and the artwork there made this look like it had come from a third-rate museum.

"A whiskey?" he asked, pouring himself one into a crystal glass.

"Please," she said.

"This is a thankless job sometimes," he mused, half to himself.

"I'm sure it is," she said.

"Do you know that every time I come to Los Angeles, half my time is spent meeting actors and other entertainers?"

"It must be tedious," she said.

He turned and faced her, a glass in each hand. "They are either idiots or intellectuals, and always ineffectual outside the one area in which they excel. And yet they each have a totally disproportionate sphere of influence and must be catered to. One of life's little puzzles, hmm?"

He lifted his glass, took a sip, and smacked his lips appreciatively. "We have a problem, Erica. A big problem," he said.

He brought her glass over. She took it and watched him return to his seat. He sighed as he lowered himself down, then took another sip of his scotch.

She did the same. Although not normally a scotch drinker, she appreciated the smoky peat flavor. Single-malt, it probably cost five hundred dollars a bottle, maybe more.

"We're sweeping the streets," she said. "The city's never seen a roundup like this before. The net will catch something, I assure you."

Englund did not look impressed. "Whichever way you look at it, we have a problem," he reiterated.

"Well, at least the media is muzzled," she said. "As far as everyone is concerned, White has gone to his new life overseas."

"The New York reception had to be canceled. Didn't look good," he said. He picked up a glossy sheet of paper from a pile on the intricately carved table beside his chair. "And then there are these, of course."

"We have our network people discrediting them," she said.

He looked down at the poster. The photograph had been taken from a rooftop, he presumed. It showed the burning limousine, the other one a short distance away, the approaching men with raised hands protecting their faces, the flames leaping up to a black cloud of smoke.

The caption below said: "Cap White's funeral pyre."

"A picture is worth a thousand words," Englund intoned softly. "They're all over the city, you know. Pasted up on every wall and pole."

"The network is going to run a film of Cap White on a beach in Europe. The editors are working on it now."

"And who will the people believe?" he said. "That's the question, isn't it?"

Strom looked uncomfortably into her glass.

"The Board is very upset about this," he continued. "They want heads to roll—you know that, don't you?"

"Yes," she said. "The detail guarding White are all out on the street, stripped of rank and privilege."

"More important heads," he said meaningfully.

She looked up at him, the first evidence of fear in her taut silence.

"I can only protect you so far," he said. "My umbrella is limited in the shadow it can cast."

He drained his scotch and said, "Aaah." Then he looked at her for a long moment before speaking. "What would you do in my place?" he asked.

"Reprimand me and let me get on with the job," she said, the first sign of certainty entering her voice. "I will get it done."

Englund nodded. "Do you know what you're dealing with here, Erica?"

Something in his tone, a thoughtfulness, made her remain silent.

"It's not just the Night Whistlers, not just a band of well-organized Devos. Not at all." He rose and poured another slug of scotch into his glass. Turning, he leaned an elbow on the liquor cabinet and swirled the drink in his glass, regarding it with seeming fascination.

"What we are seeing here," he continued somberly, "are the seeds of the Second American Revolution."

He went back to his chair and sat down. "Do you know your history, Erica?"

"Just what I learned in school," she replied.

"Ah, yes, the revisionist history. Well, I'm sure it will come as no surprise to you that it was modified extensively to . . . let us say, support the Corporate viewpoint. The fact is, a ragtag militia of unorganized colonists overcame the greatest power in the world. How? This, one of the wealthiest new countries in the world, was reserved for the elite, but things got out of control. It became a populist nation. Ever hear of Patrick Henry? 'Is life so dear, or peace so sweet, as to be purchased at the price of chains and slavery? Forbid it, Almighty God. I know not what course others may take, but as for me, give me liberty or give me death!' Rhetoric like that inflamed this nation. A handful of men was all it took to start the embers burning."

"What's that got to do with here and now?" Strom asked.

"Ideas, Erica. Ideas have power. There was an idea called communism in the last century. A stupid, unworkable system, but it almost conquered the world, until it was brought down by another even more simple idea: freedom. Yes, 'give me liberty or give me death' is a very powerful idea, and it is the idea that motivates these Whistlers of yours. It has always motivated men. Always will. Do you see? Wherever there is centralized power, what some might call injustice, these ideas have the ground in which to flourish. We live in a world of limited resources. There are not enough for everyone. Those who rise to the top can lay claim to what there is. That is the position we occupy. That is the way it has to be, do you see? But it also leaves us open to attack."

Strom nodded.

"These people—Gray and his so-called rabble—are very, very dangerous, and the Board is very concerned about them," Englund said. "Now do you see why?"

Again she nodded.

"Good," he said. "Do your job and you have the chance to be a hero. Fail . . . Well, you understand, don't you?"

Strom gulped the remainder of her drink and resisted the urge to cough.

CHAPTER 13

While Erica Strom was facing her Corporate master, John Gray sat forty feet below the surface of Third Street in a small dank cavern that had once been a shunting area for heavy equipment. Lead-colored railroad tracks gleamed softly in the dim light, and rusting metal rods protruded from pockmarked walls. A faint odor of oil permeated everything. Coincidentally, Erica Strom was the subject of the conversation conducted among the Whistler inner circle.

"The bitch is moving on the whole city," Maggie Sharp said tightly.

"Yas," Jackie Arbunckle drawled. "But she also pissing off dis city, and dat can only help us."

"And how many has she picked up so far?" Maggie snapped. "Three, four?"

"Low-level, nobody important," Jackie countered.

"Everyone's important," Maggie said.

In contrast to this exchange, Gray again remained entirely silent—half reclining against filthy brickwork, his eyes fixed on the middle space, on the gloom. To Gray's left, also silent, sat Klein. His eyes, however, were fixed on the Steyr M-17 in his hands. Four feet across the perpetually damp concrete, young Paolo Cruz looked troubled, eyes traveling from one face to another. Also present was a worried Malcolm Cobb, but then the pale weapons master always looked worried.

"What exactly is the damage?" Gray interjected finally. He looked at Maggie. "Alvarez in Echo Park was picked up. Who was the other?"

"Ben Yoo in Westwood. He carries for us," she said. "Picks up things once and a while."

"How far down the chain?"

"A long way," she said. She looked at a spot on the wall. "I know him, though."

"But does he know you?"

She shook her head. "No, not really."

"And nobody's accessible to us?"

"Not unless we plan on hitting the Towers again," she said.

"Could do it, you know," Danny said softly. He laid the rifle against his knee. "Not at Trans Global, but hit them just the same. Somewhere where they're not looking for it."

"They gotta be stick men all over the place, you know," Jackie said.

"Sure, stick men," whispered Maggie. "So you take down a stick man. Who's gives a fuck? I mean, who cares we take out some small-change ass-kicker?"

Arbunckle looked at the little red-haired girl. "Hey, blood's blood, sister. We hit some guy, and suddenly people know. You follow? Dey *know* dat we's around."

"No, they won't," Gray said, and something in his voice silenced the cavern, so that even Klein glanced up from his weapon.

Gray stood up, a long tube in one hand, a tool-kit box in the other. "We can't go small on this one. We can't just start taking out the rank and file. We got to think big, very big. We have to show them that there's nothing worse than force that just keeps getting stronger the more you're trying to knock it down. You understand? Just keeps getting stronger."

It was almost palpable how the mood in the room changed. Interest lighted every face. Paolo even smiled.

"We're going to hit them where they're not looking for it. Where they have never dreamed of being hit," he said. "And while we do it, we're also going to increase our effectiveness threefold. Maybe quadruple it."

He put the tool box on a stool and opened the lid, lifting out stacks of neatly packed cards. "I have here three hundred idents waiting for a fingerprint and a name. Nameless, faceless, waiting to be filled by a whole new generation of Whistlers."

He opened one end of that cardboard tube and tapped it until a piece of paper protruded. Laying the tube aside, he unrolled the paper and slowly stepped to a wooden wall beam. Then, finally stabbing the ends of the paper through a nail, he slowly let it all unfurl—a crude map, but nonetheless discernible, with a road, buildings, fences, a river bed, a track, mountains in the distance.

"We're going back to the beginnings," John Gray said, his face as cold as rock. "We are going back to where it all started: the Mojave Correctional Facility."

CHAPTER 14

Annie Fumito had made a conscious decision not to succumb to the encroaching disease of apathy. Instead she became a spirit living in a body and constantly watched for a sign that would end the nightmare.

"Something is going to happen. . . . One day you'll get a sign. Follow it," Marcie had said. And for some reason Annie believed her.

And so she watched and waited, not knowing what she was looking for. She gazed into the eyes of both prisoners and guards, hoping to see something there. She listened to snatches of conversation, alert for a key word or phrase. She looked at the shapes of rocks on the ground, at the face of the moon, at circling hawks and the camp dogs. She scrutinized everything for this sign, this something she could follow out of Mojave. And, as time passed, she began to see things very clearly.

Every face had a luminosity, no matter how prosaic in appearance; every object had its own kind of lucidity, a shape so uniquely its own, that it seemed to pulsate with life. She also began, at times, to know the thoughts of people around her, as if they were sentences, written on their faces or in the aura that surrounded them.

Once she sensed that someone was about to die—an old lady who worked in the guards' laundry. One afternoon, Annie looked at her, as usual, watching for a sign, and she knew the woman would never see another sunrise. She had no idea how she knew; the thought just came to her. But it had a clarity and force that was undeniable. When she heard the next day that the woman had died that night, she was not surprised.

What did in a sense surprise her was that none of this surprised her. The intensification of her perceptions had become as natural as breathing.

Nor did it surprise Marcie.

"You got a choice of closing down or opening up," Marcie said one day when Annie explained her feelings. "The ones that close down are the walking dead. It's just a matter of time before they fall. The ones that open up, they're the survivors. Like me. And like you, kid. I saw that in you from the beginning."

Marcie never talked again about being a spirit to survive, but she did talk about survival to the girl. "The day I knew I would survive this camp was the day I knew I was willing to face anything," she said. "I knew that whatever they did to me, no matter how vicious, that I could face it and I would survive it. From that point on, I never backed down to nobody. And believe me, kid, they know when you're that way. They leave you alone. They know."

Marcie generally came to Annie in the evenings, skirting the edge of the marshaling yard where executions were held at least twice a month and the wind through the chain link suggested the last breaths. For the most part, she mostly just listened to the woman's stories; fragments of memories from the last twenty years were etched in her memory, and there was not much she had missed. She would tell tales of the camp. After a while of listening to these tales of the camp, Annie began to feel as if she too had spent the past two decades behind these barbed-wire fences.

She heard of the guard, Basil, who had run amok one day and killed four prisoners and three other guards before being shot down. There was "Fish" Baker, over in the men's quarters, who had poured cleaning fluid all over his clothes and immolated himself, sitting cross-legged in the center of the exercise field. There was the female guard, Diedre, who used to do inspections with a plastic dildo strapped to her waist. She used it on a different victim each night. Until the morning came when they found her dead, eyes bulging, the dildo forced all the way down her throat. A mild little Korean girl named Kim, who turned out to be a tae kwan do expert, had been executed for the crime.

Marcie told her about the escape attempts, including the one soon after she arrived at Mojave of a thin young boy named Johnny. "I'll never forget his eyes. I told him he couldn't give up and he looked at me and said, 'What gave you the idea that I'm ready to give up?' I never saw eyes like that before. You believed them.

"He had a cat when he arrived, and it escaped and lived just outside the perimeter. Hilda the black matron took him out with her one night to call the cat so she could waste it and also to have her little bit of fun with him—she liked them young. He got her gun and blew her away and took off across the desert with the cat."

"Did they catch him?" Annie asked.

Marcie smiled. "Couldn't find him. Tried to say some bones out there were his, but they weren't. No, my friend Johnny was one of the few to get away. Maybe the only one to make it. I know he did."

Annie didn't ask how Marcie knew, for she too knew things. She was beginning to understand knowing.

The other prisoners, she noticed, were beginning to regard her strangely. Not with the awe in which they held Marcie, of course, but with something approaching it. They whispered about her, she knew. One woman told her she was "touched." It was a compliment. They even came to her for advice now and then. Problems in the camp were limited, usually mundane and ordinary, but they were the only problems the inmates had, and they made the most of them. They had to do with relationships, status, illnesses, fears, and what had been lost. Annie had what some perceived as serenity and, consequently, they thought she also had answers. She did not, but she listened kindly enough and, in most cases, that seemed to be all that was needed.

Even the TS dyke Bruiser seemed to have given up her sexual aspirations. In truth, this reprieve probably had more to do with Marcie than anything else. One night, while Annie had been sitting in Marcie's room, the trustee had pushed her puglike face into the door and leered down at her. "You gonna share that young stuff or keep it all to yourself, Marcie?" Bruiser had asked.

Marcie had risen from her bed and walked to the door, stopping inches away from Bruiser's face. "You ever touch her and they'll find you hanging from the wire by those things you call tits," she'd hissed softly.

Bruiser turned pale. That she believed what Marcie said

was obvious. She had avoided even looking at Annie since that night.

Annie thanked Marcie for her intercession.

"I hate that cunt," was all Marcie said.

Daily life at Mojave was no different from what it had always been: remorselessly routine. Up at dawn, your own regulation wash rag dipped into a bucket shared by twenty women, a small bowl of gruel, and a cup of coffee so weak it barely discolored the water, then on to your work assignment. Lunch would be turnips or some kind of cactus soup. Dinner would be more of the same, although sometimes potatoes miraculously appeared—a special treat.

According to Marcie, when she had first arrived the only work activity was building more sheds to house more prisoners, manufacturing the parts needed to build them, and digging graves for dead prisoners. Sporadic building still occurred, and they had a crematorium for the dead, but after a few years some cost-conscious Corporate figure freak decided that the profit motive should apply to this outpost as well, and now the inmates were used to make engine parts and tools. There was also a printing facility, where huge machines cranked out billions of government forms. Work details varied. For the most part, male inmates would operate the machinery, while women would do the piece work and cleanup. It was the only time men and women met; during meals and at night, they were segregated.

Annie found that, with her heightened awareness, even the routine had its own special sense of uniqueness. There was a rhythm to everything, she discovered: the grinding and pounding of machinery, the muttered conversations, the motions of guards, the shuffling of feet and the darting of fearful eyes. It all formed a kind of harmony, a ballet of sound and motion, through which she floated while watching and waiting.

She grew sensitive to discordancies, for they always signaled a divergence from routine. Not the discordancies of a guard's shout or swift blow or an inmate fainting from heat and malnutrition. No, they were part of the harmony. The discordancies she saw were far subtler and less obvious.

There were the discordancies of nature, such as a camp dog growling for no reason, bristles rising at some invisible foe, the sudden appearance of buzzards on the camp perimeter, an increased activity among armies of ants, the strange shrieking of the wind. And then there were those of people: an unexpectedly reserved expression never noted before on the face of an inmate, a stumbling guard who falls to his knees after tripping on a pail, a meaningless non-sequitur remark.

At first Annie thought of them as omens. Everyone in the camp believed in omens, luck, the fate of the draw, predestination, and a dozen similar theories. But as she grew aware of the rhythm of things, she began to see them as nothing but discordancies, a divergence from the pattern that would swirl events into a different direction.

The ants, for instance.

She had been watching them for days, a thin line that came from a hole in the ground and treked into their hut, across the floor and then down below the floorboards to find whatever it was they sought. And then, on one particular day, their number multiplied by a dozen. The line was thick and frenzied. It was no longer a determined march but a mad, disorganized rush.

She knew that the rhythm had changed and she walked through the day with her senses outstretched. When the gunfire erupted that night in the men's quarters and whining flechettes filled the air, she lay in bed and nodded to herself, while the others rushed to the windows.

Twelve male inmates were killed that night. Two had tried to escape by overpowering a guard, and the other guards had reacted in an indiscriminate frenzy of murder. The next day the ants had gone.

On this particular day—a Sunday, someone told her—she was walking from the print shop to a warehouse, pushing a cart loaded with requisition forms, when she felt a change in the rhythm. It was midmorning, and already the sun was lashing down at the camp, rising waves of heat warping vision.

She allowed the cart to roll to a stop on the concrete path and stood stock still, straining her ears, squinting her eyes at nothing in particular, stretching every sense she had outward—beyond the path, the building she was approaching, out beyond the camp perimeter and into the wilted desert.

Nothing.

But she wasn't wrong. She knew that.

A string of inmates moved from one building to another, scuffling in the heat, shoulders bowed. A guard yelled for them to move faster.

Two men in cool white suits talked to each other in front of the administration building.

Two female inmates entered the guard recreation center, a long low building with a satellite dish on the roof.

A truck coughed from the warehouse to the first perimeter gate and creaked to a halt as two guards sauntered from their shelter to inspect it.

A guard in the tower nearest to her coughed.

And then she saw it, one of the camp dogs. A doberman, coming fast from the perimeter fence, head low and swinging from side to side, sleek black body taut. It moved at a trot, coming in a line that would take it ten feet away from her.

The dog was moving with some kind of crazed intention, driven by the need to discover.

What? She didn't know, but slowly she moved over so that their paths would intersect.

It happened in a moment. The animal passed within a foot of her, allowing a glimpse of a dripping pink tongue and baleful golden eyes.

Its passing engulfed her in waves of what she could only think of as energy. She closed her eyes and, as she felt them, actually read them, she knew the dog was insane with worry, close to total panic.

When she opened her eyes again, the dog had already passed between the buildings, heading out across an open lot of sand to the other side of the perimeter to continue its search.

For what? She didn't know. All she was left knowing was that a strange excitement gripped her, the likes of which she had never felt before.

Annie walked through the day in a fever of vigilance, seeing like she had never seen before. She read faces like books, and the thoughts of others were like reflections in distant mirrors, totally visible, yet lacking definition unless she moved closer.

She was charged, vibrating faster than a human eye could see.

She knew something was going to happen. She knew also that this discordancy today was somehow different from the others, more immediate, more powerful. She knew that it was the herald of something truly momentous—the sign she had always been waiting to appear.

By late afternoon nothing had happened. She didn't care. Her intensity didn't dip or flag.

Other people began to notice. There was a young boy in the print shop. Maybe a year older than she was, his name was David. Thin, dark, with a wild shock of black hair and hungry brown eyes, he often watched her. Usually he smiled when he saw her, a quick flash of teeth that was gone before anyone else noticed. Sometimes he spoke, just a word or two. A greeting, a question.

This afternoon when she felt his gaze on her she turned to meet it. He walked over, carrying a box of paper, and slowed as he reached her. "What's the matter with you?" he asked out of the side of his mouth.

"What?" she asked.

"You're different. Something's different."

All she could do was nod. He moved on and then looked back, a puzzled frown on his forehead.

Just before sunset, the print foreman gave her a sheaf of papers to take to the administration building. When she got outside the air was heavy, the sun a sinking red ball, bleeding all over the desert.

As she got to the offices she heard the noise on the road outside the perimeter. It was a bus, maybe two—a new load of inmates from the city.

Quickly she moved from the road and walked twenty feet up the concrete path to the double front doors. She went in and took the papers to the desk. The guard, a thin woman with gray hair named Edna, didn't look up.

"Excuse me," Annie said. "These are for Officer Freund, from the print foreman."

Edna looked up with a frown, her eyes unfocused. "Down the hall, third door on the left. If he's not there, put them on his desk," she said, inclining her head.

Annie went down the hall. A door at the end opened and Warden Tull came out. He wore a well-pressed uniform and black boots as usual. With him was Edmund Fishback, the head of the guards, a squat, short man with balding black hair and bristle ringing his face.

"I've had the request in for more staff for six weeks now," the warden was grumbling. Neither man even looked at her as they passed her in the hall.

She went into the third door and found an empty office. Quickly she put the papers on the desk and turned to leave.

"Wait," Edna said when Annie reached her desk.

Annie stopped there.

"What's your name?" the guard asked.

"Annie," she replied.

Edna nodded, then bent down to her papers again. For a moment, Annie stood there, then realized she was dismissed.

When she reached the front doors of the office, the two buses had pulled up. Hull and Fishback stood on the edge of the circular road, waiting to greet the new arrivals.

She should have gone on, returned as fast as she could to the print shop. But instead she stopped on the path, about eight feet behind the two men, hardly daring to breathe.

She had to watch. She had to.

The pneumatic doors of both buses whooshed open and the prisoners began to spill out. Guards came out of the building behind her, but she might have been invisible, for they moved past, swinging their guns, and began to herd the prisoners into lines.

"Move it! Get in line there! Welcome to the Last Resort!" The same cries she had heard just weeks earlier.

It was the usual ragged bunch, stinking of fear. Mostly middle-aged, some in their twenties, a couple of real old ones, male, female, only one girl as young as herself. Apathetic for the most part, eyes downcast and furtive.

Except for one.

Front row, second from the end on the left.

Her eyes locked on him and her face began to burn.

There was nothing distinguishing about him. He wore blue jeans and sneakers. He was of medium height and slight build. He had raven hair. His face was still.

He was very different from the others.

For one thing, Annie knew that he was completely relaxed, not a fiber of strain in his body. For another, he was *watching and seeing*.

When his eyes reached her they had the force of a physical blow, even though from this distance she couldn't even really see them. She stood there, unable to move, entranced, her perceptions like the hairs on the back of a scared cat, screaming some message so loudly she couldn't hear it.

Tull broke the spell. He stepped forward and went into his usual routine. "My name is Warden Hank Tull the Second and my job, among other things, is to welcome you to our humble abode."

Annie stumbled forward then, almost losing her balance. Righting herself, she began to walk forward, purposefully yet casually. She turned left behind the warden and walked along the edge of the road, her eyes straight ahead while his voice droned on behind her.

But she couldn't help herself. When she knew she was in front of the stranger she stopped as if to adjust her shoes and turned to look at him.

His eyes were fixed on her. Expressionless and calm, they were eyes unlike any she had seen before. Dark, they seemed to stretch infinitely back. And far back in their endless depths, a quiet flame flickered. They were the eyes of some kind of phantom man.

She felt a wash of fear but realized almost simultaneously that although those eyes carried that message for some, it was not for her.

She straightened up, tore herself away from his grip, and began to walk away.

She wanted to scream, to jump, to do something to release the clangor of emotion swirling inside her. For she knew that something was going to happen. She had just seen her sign.

CHAPTER 15

When Annie looked out of her window before going to sleep, the moon was full and round behind wispy layers of cloud. It seemed alive, that moon, pulsating with energy and swinging ever so slightly from side to side.

She had avoided going to Marcie's room, as she normally did, her feelings too intense to share—even with Marcie. Nor did she think she could actually express them very clearly. At least not verbally. Inside, however, they had coagulated into a pulsating core of hope and wonder.

Something was going to happen.

The next morning, the first chance she had to look for him was when she went to the print shop, hoping it had been his assigned area. Breakfast, such as it was, was a segregated affair—men over at their side of the camp, women on theirs. There was no sign of the man—her phantom—nor any of the other new inmates.

She asked David, the young boy who worked in the print shop, what had happened to the new arrivals. It was a whispered conversation behind a twenty-foot stack of paper sheets.

"They're probably in the holding cells, waiting to be processed," he said. After a curious look at her he said, "Why? You know someone there?"

She shook her head and said unsatisfyingly, "No. I was just curious."

He appeared as if he were going to press it, but he didn't. Instead he dropped his eyes and said, "You're really pretty." He looked up, his brown eyes defiant, as if the words had been dragged from him.

Annie was momentarily speechless. Since coming to the camp, nothing had been farther from her mind than sex—unless it had been on occasion to avoid the attentions of other female inmates and guards. Between men and women it was impossible, unthinkable.

"Oh . . . thank you," she stammered.

"I wish . . . I wish things were different," he said.

She felt what he was feeling then: his liking, perhaps even desire, for her, his confusion, desperation, and, above all, his stifling hopelessness.

"They will be," she said fiercely. "You've got to believe it. One day soon, they will be."

He looked up at her in surprise, and the dawning of another expression in his eyes: hope.

"What the fuck you doing?"

The voice jolted them both. Moving fast at them was Blackjack Staples, one of the more vicious guards. He reached David and placed a massive hand around the back of his neck.

A hulk of a man with an IQ smaller than his shoe size, Blackjack had thick dark eyebrows, a booming voice, and a body all of 6´ 4˝ tall and 320 pounds in weight.

"Think it's party time?" he said, effortlessly shaking David back and forth. "Looking for some solitary time, huh?"

David glared up at him.

"Leave him alone!" Annie flashed.

"Huh?" the guard said, bemused by this spirited defiance.

"Leave him alone. He wasn't doing anything. I was just asking him where the transparency folio paper was," she said, making up words.

"What?" Blackjack asked, but he loosened his grip on the boy.

"The transparency folio."

"Well . . . well, get a fucking move on," Blackjack said, and he released David.

Annie and David walked quickly away between the paper stacks. "Transparency folio paper!" David said under his breath. As soon as they turned the corner he broke into laughter.

"It's all I could think of," Annie protested.

"Hey, it worked."

They had to separate and get back to their work stations.

"I'll see you later," David said, and he turned right between another stack.

"Let me know what you hear about the new prisoners," Annie called after him.

"Sure," he said over his shoulder.

She talked to Marcie that night.

"You've been . . . somewhere else," Marcie said.

Annie felt her spine stiffen. She still wasn't willing to share her knowing with anyone else.

They sat in Marcie's room. In the background the radio played Corporate songs.

"What do you mean?" Annie asked.

Marcie wrinkled her freckled nose. "Sweetie, I don't understand you, but I do know you. You didn't come by last night, and all day you've been walking around like a bolt of electricity waiting to blast off in a streak of lightning. I'm not the only one who noticed it. So, what's going on?"

Marcie was on the bed, Annie on the only chair. She fell back and drew her knees up and buried her face in them.

"Come on," Marcie said.

Annie looked up, at the still strong face, the pale blue eyes, the woman who had inspired her to survive.

"I saw the sign," she whispered.

"What?"

"You told me once that I'd see a sign that would show me the way out of here. I saw it. I really did."

Marcie shook her head. "That was a pep talk, kid."

Annie's eyes were bloodshot, her voice harsh. "No, it wasn't," she said.

Marcie just stared at her.

"You know more than you think. More than you'll admit," Annie said, and her voice was remorseless. "You've tapped into the vein of truth, but a part of you still denies it. You can't. There's going to come a time when you can't."

"What the fuck are you talking about?" Marcie said, a forced amusement in her voice.

Annie pushed herself up from the chair. "You know," she said. And she walked out of the room.

She saw him the next day. In the print shop. He was pushing a trolley of paper from one of the machines, across the floor to the pallet loading area.

The first thing she noticed was his presence. The second

thing she noticed was his economy of motion. Nothing was wasted. He moved like people she had once seen on television, in something called a ballet. It was pure grace. It was power.

She watched him and saw things others would not have seen. She saw that he was driven by a terrible resolve. And she saw that somewhere deep in his being was a hidden place so painful, so forbidding, he never entered it, or let others see it.

And then, while she looked at his disappearing back, he suddenly stopped and turned and locked his eyes on hers. Something like a smile flitted across his mouth before he turned and moved on.

Phantom man! she thought.

She wondered what he had seen. A small, thin Oriental girl, the bones of her face protruding from malnutrition, black eyes and black hair, long and matted. Just another inmate, filthy and exhausted and fearful. Was that what he saw? She thought not, for he was another watcher and saw things most people didn't.

She saw him a few more times during the morning, but he appeared not to notice her again. He worked with complete intensity, as if aware only of what he was doing when he was doing it. She knew, however, that he was aware of much more.

In the afternoon, she saw Blackjack attempt to put the new inmate in his place. It was a ritual the guard went through with all new male prisoners, and it never varied.

"Hey, you, new meat, come here!" Blackjack bellowed. He stood in front of the guards' office, a cup of steaming coffee in his hand.

The new inmate was about ten feet away from him, pushing another pallet of paper.

Annie was about twenty feet from them both, returning from an errand to the administration building.

The new inmate pulled the pallet to a stop and looked at Blackjack.

"Yeah, you. Come here," Blackjack said.

He moved over to the guard and stopped about three feet short of him—just out of his reach, Annie noticed. She was aware of nothing else now, intent on what was happening.

Blackjack derisively looked the much smaller man over, then grinned. His eyes still on the inmate, he held his cup out and let it fall.

Hot coffee splashed over the man's feet. The plastic cup bounced once, then stopped. The man didn't move.

"Uh-oh," Blackjack said. "Clumsy me."

Still the man said nothing.

"Pick up the cup," Blackjack said, shifting his right foot back.

Annie knew what would happen now. She'd seen it before. As the victim bent for the cup, Blackjack would unleash a kick. Sometimes he went for the ribs, at times the head. The result, in either case, would be an injured inmate who knew exactly who the boss was.

She wanted to run forward and pick up the cup herself or cry out a warning, but something kept her frozen in place. She couldn't help but think her phantom knew exactly what was happening.

The man bent for the cup and Blackjack's foot swung forward.

She didn't exactly see what happened—it was too subtle. But somehow, in moving down, the man had adjusted his feet and stepped ever so slightly to the side.

Blackjack's kick lashed harmlessly into the air.

The man was upright, politely holding the cup out to the guard.

Blackjack fought to regain his balance, his face puzzled. He blinked at the inmate, trying to realize what had happened. "What's your name?" he said finally.

"Troy, sir."

"Well, Troy, take off your shirt and wipe that coffee off the floor."

"Excuse me?" the man said.

"Take off your shirt, wipe that coffee up, then put your shirt back on."

Without a change of expression, the man drew his shirt swiftly over his head and fell into a crouch, facing Blackjack's feet.

Annie sensed that he was aware of every motion of those feet as he mopped at the coffee. When he was done, he moved quickly back, wrung the shirt out in one quick motion, and slipped it back over his head.

"I didn't say to wring it out," Blackjack said belligerently.

"Sorry, I didn't think. Is there anything else, sir?" the stranger mildly asked the guard.

Blackjack smiled, his confidence regained. He'd made his point. "Just do as you're told and you'll survive—for a while. I'll be watching you. Now get back to work!"

"Yes, sir," the man said in the same polite tone he'd used all along and returned to the pallet he had been pushing.

And odd thing struck Annie then. The whole episode had taken only three or four minutes, but during that time the man had not been afraid. She could sense fear. It was something even the insensitive learned to do in Mojave. And she was not insensitive. During the entire incident, both the man's control and calm had been intact, invulnerable. He hadn't been afraid, not for a second. Odd, but for some reason not surprising.

David told her the news the next morning.

A nervous excitement swirled around him. "Did you hear what happened last night?" he asked urgently when they met in the stacks.

She shook her head.

"Blackjack. He's dead. Someone did the bastard and did him good," the boy said with satisfaction. "They found him between some sheds. He'd been doing his rounds. Someone broke his arms, his ribs—and his neck!"

"Who?" she asked, although she suddenly knew the answer.

"They don't know. They questioned us all, but for all they know it could have been another guard. I mean, Blackjack wasn't loved by anyone, probably not even by his mother, right? They have no idea. But I tell you, the heat's on. There're a bunch of pissed-off guards in Mojave today. So keep your nose clean."

"Yeah, sure, thanks," Annie said distractedly.

David looked momentarily disappointed that his news wasn't received with more of a reaction from her, but then his good humor returned. "Took the bastard apart," he said.

When she returned to the main floor, she saw her phantom almost immediately. He was loading boxes onto a wooden pallet with the same grace he always used, his face calm.

His eyes flicked over her, then returned to the task at hand.

She wondered how he had done what he had done to Blackjack but then realized it didn't matter. He was a phantom—magical—and he could probably do anything.

CHAPTER 16

Alfred Garcia liked to think of himself as the uncrowned economic czar of the east Los Angeles basin. Although the city's dwellers might not have described him quite so formidably, the man definitely represented more than just another black-market hustler. Point of fact: Not only did he control the primary hump of the basin's underground commerce, including the distribution of everything from methane to margarine, he also had his fingers in several other artificially rich pies. To manage these industries, he further employed a small army of wholly legitimate lawyers, accountants, security advisers, secretaries, word processors, and public-relations assistants—all comfortably housed on three floors of a mid-Wilshire office building . . . which he also owned.

Although of Filipino extraction, and thus dark and broad-featured, Alfred found other family antecedents more significant. His great-grandfather had been a bookmaker in the Long Beach area. His grandfather had been a slum landlord in San Pedro until property values skyrocketed and he became a very rich and respectable patron of the arts. And his father was an outwardly respectable developer of office buildings, with half the county government in his pocket. Expediency, then, was a trait common to all of them, and a trait that Alfred most definitely inherited.

Each member of his somewhat gnarled family tree had not only possessed the ability to perceive a need but also the ability to fill it. Moreover—and this may well have been the key to their success—none had been particular as to just how that need was filled.

Thus by the time the Corporate powers-that-be had managed their stranglehold on the country, and the subsequent division of profitable monopolies, Alfred had already seen and laid the groundwork for his place in history.

Monopolies, he knew, had two main characteristics: They provided their owners and/or shareholders with exorbitant profits; and they squeezed the consumer, thus creating a definite need for alternative sources of supply. Which was where he came in.

Alfred had a number of advantages over his competition— all of which had to do with the fact that his family had already amassed a fair amount of wealth. Consequently, he was a shareholder in a number of major corporations and was on very good terms with county, state, and federal government officials. He had clout—political and financial. Nor was he some street hustler starting out with a limited budget, bolstered by some initiative. He had the financing to leave the starter's gate at a gallop.

Whatever the need, his organization found a way to fill it. Indeed, about the only commodity he didn't touch was drugs—too cheap and too readily available. But if you wanted unpolluted drinking water, New Zealand lamb, a tailored wool blazer, dual chrome exhaust pipes, a .22 gas-operated pellet pistol, chemically free tomatoes, real eggs in a real shell, soyless burger meat, Highland malt scotch, Russian vodka, a fifty-foot I-beam, and a thousand other unavailable, rationed, or expensive products, Alfred was most certainly your man.

As would suit a figure of his means, Alfred lived on the beach, just north of Malibu, just south of the Armand Hammer Memorial Park and Shrine. His home, in simple terms, was magnificent: a high-walled, mock-Georgian and heavily gated estate. He also had what could be considered lesser homes in the predominantly Corporate retirement town of Santa Barbara a little farther up the coast and another down in Baja. Alfred liked the ocean.

Given that the nature of their visit was strictly business, however, Detective Wimple and Erica Strom chose to confront the man at his mid-Wilshire office.

Wimple, who had known Alfred for fifteen years, had actually once attended a party at that Malibu beach home—

replete with nubile love slaves from three continents and a veritable mountain of cheese blintzes (Alfred's favorite delicacy). Alfred, however, preferred not to conduct business at his residence. Nor did he like to discuss sensitive matters on the telephone, knowing full well that there was an entire town outside of Washington, D.C., filled with people who did nothing but monitor every telephone call in the world on a massively intrusive and powerful system known as the Octopus.

Not that Alfred had a great deal to hide from the nation's Corporate masters, for he had long maintained what he called a "give and take" relationship with Trans Global, which meant that he provided dribs and drabs of data from his informant networks in exchange for the right to conduct his business freely. But out of professional habit, he always took sensitive meetings in person.

Behind the decision to pay Mr. Garcia a visit lay a simple but fairly profound problem. Whereas Strom had been crowing about the success of her Citizens for Safety campaign, proclaiming that the Whistlers were now literally on the run, Wimple had his doubts. What, if anything, he had asked himself, would indicate that the Whistlers had even been mildly disturbed by Strom's campaign? And if disturbed, how then would they respond? He was further concerned about what he termed the temperature on the streets, which meant the *real* feelings of those population pools that Strom's campaign so depended upon.

It was in search of answers to these questions, then, that Wimple had decided to call upon Garcia. As for Strom's presence, she simply insisted upon it, stating, "I want to meet this character. Put in the personal touch. See what he's made of. Watch his reactions."

Naturally, had Wimple any choice in the matter, he would have much preferred that Strom not meet Alfred Garcia. Not only was Garcia a temperamental fellow and prone to the most obscene language imaginable, but for some thirty years now, Wimple had carefully hoarded his contacts—cultivating them, guarding them, nurturing them. Moreover, the relationship cut both ways. To the contact, be he a sixty-dollar mouthpiece on the corner of Fifth and Nowhere or the Great Garcia himself, they all knew where they stood with Wimple. He was known as an honorable cop—a contradiction in terms in most cases but not in his. Strom, on the other hand, was a wild card: With Strom anything could happen.

Alfred's secretary was thin, elegant, blond, and solicitous. She assured Detective Wimple and Chief Inspector Strom that Mr. Garcia would see them as soon as he completed a very important telephone transaction. She further offered them food and/or drinks, particularly recommending the guava juice. When offers were declined, she actually looked pained and suggested a wonderful Darjeeling tea grown in the shadows of the Himalayas.

"Nothing, thank you," Strom said firmly, while Wimple merely shook his head.

True to her word, the obliging young blonde showed them into Alfred's office seven minutes later.

In keeping with his circumstances, Alfred's office was thoroughly and ostentatiously lavish. The walls in what his decorator had described as "southwest bone" were high and ever so curved to meet the ceiling. The carpet, in Roman gold, had been carefully selected to tastefully clash with a forest-green sofa and deep leather chairs. The desk—a massive slab of black marble supported by claw-and-ball legs—was likewise in tasteful disharmony.

To complete the ambiance of sheer success, there was Alfred himself: half seated, half slouched behind that gleaming slab of marble. A slim man of average height in his midfifties, he had deceptively soft brown eyes, liquid, luminous, to offset a feline smile revealing teeth that only the prosperous could maintain. His jacket, in Manila's finest acetate, was also Roman gold, while his trousers in black spandex nicely emphasized his moderately muscular thighs. There were two rings on his left fingers, one diamond and the other laid with one of the largest rubies east of Hong Kong. The diamond in his left ear was also nothing to scoff at.

"Detective," he said, his smile showing four gold teeth. "What pure delight." Then, rising from behind that kidney-shaped marble, he slowly extended a hand before turning to Strom—not reacting at all to the grotesque mess of scar tissue that was her face.

"And Chief Inspector Strom. Your fame has preceded you. What a great, great treat to finally meet you in the *flesh*."

"It's good to see you, Alfred," Wimple replied softly—

thinking that the man was definitely the most utterly charming criminal he had ever had the pleasure to know. Even Strom seemed to briefly smile before his onslaught. Although before her encounter with that flame gun, her smiles had always been deceptive.

Alfred waved them to an alcove and to those ghastly green chairs and then offered both brandy, coffee (from Colombia, of course), "Or perhaps an excellent Darjeeling tea," he said. "If you have never tasted it, you should."

"No, thank you," Strom said.

"And how is Lourdes?" Wimple said, inquiring after Garcia's wife, remembering her as a dark beauty but apparently not beautiful enough to keep her husband from straying.

"A whirlwind of energy, involved in a thousand projects aimed at helping those less fortunate than ourselves," Garcia replied. "And does she ever stop? No, the woman never stops!"

"And your children?"

"Also, you know, very energetic and exhausting. Not that this is a problem you will appreciate for some years to come, Miss Strom, but Detective Wimple here must certainly understand. Age is unavoidable. We get slow. We get lazy. Sometimes all I wish for is the freedom to sit on a boat with a fishing line drifting over the side. But it seems the older we get the more responsibilities we have. It is a sad thing," he concluded, not looking at all sad about it.

Wimple noticed the impatient compression of Strom's mouth, but fortunately she did not open it. He had warned her of the social rituals required before getting down to brass tacks with Alfred.

"Alfred, I don't know how you can talk like that. You look younger every time I see you," Wimple said.

"You are too kind." Alfred wagged a finger almost coyly at the policeman. "But then you know I have a weakness for flattery." He smiled at Strom.

She did not smile back but cleared her throat uncomfortably.

"Of course!" Alfred exclaimed delightedly. "I forget how impatient the young are. You want to know what I have discovered, and here I am talking away like a doddering old man. Forgive me."

Strom shook her head and muttered something that sounded like "It's fine."

Alfred turned his attention back to Wimple. The softness seemed to have left his eyes, but his tone remained convivial. "Let me see now. You wanted to know about those Whistlers of the Night, yes? Well, I shall tell that I have indeed made inquiries about your Whistlers. Unfortunately, however—and I stress this from the bottom of my heart—I have only been able to find out, uh, how shall I say? A hint? A whisper? A single note of their song. And what is that? Well, only this: They have dispersed. Maybe some of the leaders have left for cooler climes. Maybe they are waiting until you people reduce the heat. Maybe, well, who knows? We can speculate. We can guess. But can we really know? I don't think so."

"I don't suppose you can be any more specific?" Wimple asked.

Alfred spread his hands. "If you want the specifics of rumors. Very well, I can give you rumors. But only rumors, which are this: Your Night Whistlers have not been seen on the boulevards for several days now. In fact, I would say that it has been very quiet."

"And those rumors concerning the Whistlers leaving the city?" Strom asked.

"Well, there are those, and you understand what sort of people I refer to here. People who are not always the most articulate or reliable. People who often tell you what they believe you *want* to hear rather than what *is* heard. If you understand my point."

"And these people say what, exactly?" Strom persisted.

"They say that maybe the Whistlers have taken a small vacation, or maybe they have simply gone to find another kind of hunting ground. Which, as I understand it, would be typical of their leader."

"Meaning John Gray?"

"Yes, meaning John Gray."

Strom hesitated, running her finger along the edge of Alfred's coffee table—made in Mexico, but definitely suggestive of a Moroccan motif.

"Let me ask you something, Mr. Garcia," she said at last. "Do you, or have you ever in the past, done business with the Whistlers?"

Alfred smiled, while his left eyebrow raised in protest. "Please, Miss Strom, do I look like the sort of person who would do business with subversives? That would suggest I was sympathetic to their cause, and after all, they are enemies of the Consortium, and where would I be without that sort of economic structure? Besides, I am not a physical man, and these Whistlers are very physical people. You understand my meaning here? They have no appreciation of supply-side economics, much less an appreciation of a firm handshake."

"And you expect me to believe that?"

Garcia smiled again, "Oh, Miss Strom. How little faith you have in me. Of course I am a Corporate man. After all, were there no Corporations, I would have no business. Why? Because I fill a need that has been created by the Corporations. If there was any change in the current stability, any change in the way business is done, there would be no need of my services. Hence, change is not in my interests, and hence, the Whistlers are not in my interest, except as they pertain to you."

"But you have nothing else concrete for us?" Wimple asked.

"I am sorry," Alfred said. "But when nothing happens there is nothing to say."

"Any more rumors, any events, no matter how small, I would be grateful if you could inform me," Wimple said.

"It will be my pleasure."

Wimple rose stiffly to his feet. "Anything at all," he emphasized.

Alfred and Strom rose as well, lingering only for a moment to examine one another's eyes. . . .

Until finally: "Miss Strom"—his hand on her arm, his lips very close to her left ear—"as you know, I have many resources. And if there is anything you need, anything I can get for you to make your stay in Los Angeles more pleasurable . . ."

"The only thing that would make it pleasurable would be John Gray's head on a platter," she said.

By the time they reached the Marauder four levels beneath the street Strom had regained her normal disposition. "Well, that was a monumental waste of time," she said.

Wimple slipped behind the wheel, keeping his gaze on the rearview mirror and the expanse of blackened concrete littered with executive vehicles: a methane Mercedes, a Porsche 90, two or three stretch limos.

"Definitely a monumental waste of time," Strom breathed again.

But this time Wimple shrugged. "Maybe, maybe not."

"What do you mean?"

"Well, things are seldom how they appear to be with Alfred. He has lots of interests."

"And what's that supposed to imply? That he's unreliable?"

Wimple turned his sad eyes on her. "Of course he's unreliable. He's a criminal."

"He makes sense," Strom said. "There has been no Whistler activity in the last few days."

Wimple grunted and said, "That we know of."

"Look," Strom said, "why don't you just say it? All right? Just say it."

A soft sigh, then: "Chief Inspector, far be it from me to criticize your program, but what exactly has it accomplished? We've pulled in a few low-level tadpoles, we've paid out some cash to informants, after losing the main one. Your people are out in the valley knocking more heads, and there's a new and quite deplorable television show on the air. Why should the Whistlers be on the run?"

"Pressure, Detective. Pressure," Strom snapped. "We may not yet have a major victory here, but time is on our side. It's called persistence. We keep up the pressure and sooner or later the door is going to open. And when it does, John Gray will be on the other side."

Wimple pressed the starter and the Marauder roared to life. When he spoke again, his voice was barely audible over the engine noise.

"Well, in that case, I wouldn't want to be the one who opens that door."

For at least ten minutes after watching the black Marauder emerge from the blacker mouth of the subterranean garage, Garcia remained at the window . . . thinking about Wimple, thinking about Strom, thinking about himself and his place in things, particularly the future.

He truly liked Wimple, and he would have said so to virtually anyone. A decent man, he would have proclaimed. And he would have added, with a sense of almost paternal pride, that he was not only a man with a rare sense of honesty, but he had an understanding of realism, of what really happened in the world, that probably made him altogether a dangerous man.

Strom, on the other hand, was another case entirely. He'd

heard a lot about her from his informants in the department. "Nitro bitch" was the most common descriptive phrase. "Greased pain" was another. But even her worst critics had entirely missed the crucial point.

In fact, she was a killer. It had been obvious to him the moment he saw her. Very intelligent within certain set parameters, but undoubtedly a killer. It was both her strength and her blind spot—a callous disregard for life.

If she wasn't working for Trans Global, she'd be working for someone less legal, someone like him, perhaps. In either case, she would be valued as the hired gun she was. Her vaunted efficiency, her reputation for getting the job done, which had preceded her arrival in Los Angeles, was because of her single-minded ruthlessness. But it was also her weakness, for it had no grounding in any understanding of history, nor the future that stretched out ahead. It was simple expediency.

Alfred was a student of history. His library in the vaulted basement of his home consisted almost entirely of illegal works such as *The Power Elite, The Rise and Fall of the Third Reich*, and all fifteen volumes of Durant. And what had it taught him? That the past determined the future. And that if history determined the future, it meant the future of Strom and her masters was limited.

It might take five years, ten, even a hundred. But that was nothing in the vastness of the inexorable march of history. The fact was, it would happen. Events had been initiated, and from these events—from the intrinsic and undeniable power they had started to unleash—the future would roll along its preordained path.

A student, a businessman, an opportunist, Alfred was above all a pragmatist. Too pragmatic to ignore the course of history. True, change was not in his interests, but it was also unavoidable. And not to be ignored.

He turned from the window and returned to his desk. Sitting, he reached for the telephone and dialed the call-box number he had memorized.

It rang three times and then stopped. Although there was no sound, he knew the person on the other end was waiting for him to speak.

"Message delivered," Alfred said, and hung up.

CHAPTER 17

The Figueroa Armory, situated on the street of the same name near downtown Los Angeles, once housed an organization known as the YMCA. During the civil riots of 2010, however, the premises were taken over by the then National Guard and utilized as an emergency field hospital. During those bloody months when American liberty finally took the bullet in its heart, the building had been littered with wounded civilians—some suffering from the effects of conventional weapons, others from the flame guns, gas, and what medics came to call "sound and electrical trauma" as delivered by the Hitachi antiriot systems. When the bloodshed finally came to an end, the Figueroa facility briefly served as an interrogation center and then at last as an armory.

It was a dour place of gray walls, reinforced steel doors, and barred windows. Here and there, however, were traces of a former elegance in the fluted moldings and long-forgotten faces cut into the frieze. What had once been a swimming pool now housed rusting scrap steel and rotting timber. What had been once a racketball court now housed heaps of dead ammunition crates and boxes of requisition slips. To discourage intruders, the surrounding chain-link fence had been equipped with razor wire, while the entrances had been fitted with sensor alarms. Plans to install hot grids across the main corridor, however, had slipped into one of the bureaucratic holes that so characterized twenty-first-century life.

Although ostensibly maintained as emergency supply depots for the Urban Disturbance Teams, all such facilities were, in fact, under Trans Global jurisdiction. After a complicated process of accounting steps, the money paid for these weapons by the military and police came out of national and local government pockets (i.e., the taxpayer) and ended in Corporate coffers.

Needless to say, all weaponry and affiliated equipment was nothing less than state of the art: polycarbonate Gillette M-90s, Steyr M-17 Advanced Combat Rifles (with integrated laser sightings, of course), and Bic-60 flame pistols. There were additionally some twenty-five thousand rounds of internally propelled saboted-flechettes and another five thousand "Snap and Sizzle" M-250 fragmentation grenades. In the event of larger disruptions, officers of the Urban Disturbance Teams could requisition Arafat-Timex shoulder-launched missiles (said to be capable of honing in on a man's heartbeat). In the event of a genuinely organized uprising, there were further Porsche-Polaroid anti-armor missiles, canisters of Dowbentz neural gas, and a Flash Burn cannon from the people of Nikon-Tot. Finally, there were also the peripheral supplies, including Hitachi body armor, uniforms, medical kits, rations, tents, backpacks, and everything else a happy camper would need.

As did all the Los Angeles basin armories, the Figueroa site retained a regular guard of twenty-two men, twenty-four hours a day. A fortified outer wall had been constructed around the two primary entrances to create a defensible courtyard, with loading bays for trucks. There were, however, no major gun emplacements on the roof, and, as Gray had remarked, "Routine breeds carelessness."

Whistlers had watched the armory on random days for nearly three months: from the rust-eaten roof of an abandoned warehouse nearby, from behind the smoked glass of an office building across the street, through night-vision glasses from the grass-topped landfill that rose into the sky half a mile behind the building, and from the inside of dusty panel vans. They had taken films and taken notes. A loose-lipped guard in a drugged stupor had described the inside of the building and the security system. And by the end of his study, Gray probably knew the routine as well as the guards—perhaps better, for they had observed all three shifts in twenty-four-hour periods.

The routine seldom varied—except when outsiders entered the building.

There was only one gate, with two guards on duty at all times. Entrance was electronically controlled. Anyone who worked in the building entered with a plastic card and encoded-number ID, inserted into a computerized lock just outside the gate. All others needed Corporate, Trans Global, military, or LAPD ID, preapproved first with paperwork and then through telephone arrangements—all of which Gray had been acutely conscious of, owing to Billy Casey's work with telephone- and radio-transmission links.

And which was why, on the first moonless night in May, a seemingly drunken derelict stepped from the sidewalk in front of a military panel van barely two blocks from the armory.

Then, even before the brakes finished squealing, two shadows emerged from the blackness and went down on both the driver and his assistant with XR50 stun guns.

John Gray and Jackie Arbunckle, in olive coveralls, replete with Division insignia, lifted the bodies out of the truck neither roughly nor gently, then slid onto the vinyl seats. The suddenly sober derelict extracted both identification badges and passed them through the window.

Arbunckle said something: "You got eighteen minutes from here." But whether it was directed toward Gray or the now alert derelict was unclear. Also, more weapons were withdrawn at this point: two slightly modified Astoria machine pistols with flash suppressors and silencers.

Gray doused the lights twice before easing his foot down on the accelerator, while Arbunckle glanced at the identification cards to insure that there had been no changes since the ones they had copied.

"I say, we be fine," he whispered, while Gray again nodded but said nothing.

Three minutes and fifty-four seconds later they drew up before the Figueroa Armory gates.

There were two officers in the plexiglass booth: obviously bored, obviously counting hours, apparently half watching *The Johnny Todd* hour on a Sonitron portable. While the taller of the two officers reached for the telephone, the squat one said something like "Hey, now that's what I like." Finally, after another minute and nineteen seconds, the taller guard sauntered out to the crash gate.

He was a vaguely birdlike creature, pushing forty, but still not over the hill. In addition to his name tag, he wore a Corporate "Good Guy," pin, and what looked like a marksman's award. When Arbunckle eased open the door to meet him, he said, "You guys want coffee?"

But Arbunckle simply shook his head. "No time now with what we be doing tonight."

"Yeah." The guard sighed. "Let's take a look." He held his hand out between the bars of the gate.

Jackie slid the sealed packet of Divisional orders, gray-green to indicate priority, and the lanky officer gave them a studied glance. "And ID?"

Arbunckle lifted the ID out of his pocket and flashed it at the guard.

Another studied glance, then another sleepy smile. "Okay, pull her on in and load her out."

"No load, mon. We here to pick up, not take in."

The officer shrugged. "Hey, no difference on this end. Just bring it in when the gates open and stop at that white line." The guard pointed at a spot twenty feet behind where he stood.

"Sure thing, mon," Jackie said with another grin, then casually returned to the van.

"Piece o' cake," he said as he slipped in beside Gray. "De mon wants you to drive to de white line."

The gates swung open with squeals of rusting steel, and Gray pulled the van forward as indicated. When the gates closed again, he said softly, "Don't take anything for granted. You understand."

He sat, hands relaxed on the wheel, until the guard appeared at the window and requested his ID. As he handed it over, he noticed the other guard emerge from that plexiglass booth, an M-90 in his hands.

The guard returned Gray's ID, then nodded toward the rear of the van. "How about a regulation once-over?"

As Gray opened his door, Jackie did the same, and they both stepped out onto the oil-smeared pavement.

"Hey, mon." Arbunckle grinned as the second officer drew in sight, that M-90 still in his hands. In response, the young officer merely nodded, eyes shifting from Arbunckle to Gray, then back to the rear of the truck.

He was in his twenties, medium height, athletic build. Hair as fair as Gray's. Pale blue eyes. He looked bored, no less bored than his partner.

"I hate de night shift," Jackie was saying as Gray led the other guard to the back of the van and opened the double doors.

The man stepped forward to look inside, obscured by the open doors.

"What's that?" the guard said, nodding to what looked like some sort of screenless receiver, with more than four feet of stainless steel antennae.

"Mobile radio frequency modulator," Gray said, and then without hesitating or telegraphing the move in any way, he brought his left elbow up in a cutting jab to the officer's jaw.

As the officer slumped forward, half in the van and half out, Gray hit him a second time, then turned his attention to the modulator. The hum immediately rose to a whine.

As of that second, Bill Casey's bag of microwave tricks was scrambling the video monitor on top of the guardhouse and all radio transmissions to and from the armory.

There was a slightly awkward moment as the second guard, clearly sensing a problem, attempted to stumble back to the booth. Yet even as he began to move, Arbunckle had raised the electric stun gun: fifty-thousand volts in a twenty-degree arc.

The officer fell without a sound, crumpling in stages while his left arm shivered at his side.

"Go!" Gray said. "Go," and Jackie sprinted for the guardhouse.

A moment later the gates swung open again and an armorplated van appeared from the road.

By the time it reached the gate and started to follow them, Gray and Jackie were back in their van and moving fast down the roadway to the big loading dock in the front of the building.

Now the noise didn't matter. It was all speed.

Both vans revved, then skidded to a stop parallel to the dock.

The back of the second van opened and eight or nine people spilled out—Maggie Sharp, Malcolm Cobb, and more— all heavily armed except for Cobb, who carried only a gas-powered Ruger-Daisho pistol in one hand.

• • •

Since its inception in the planning stages, Gray had decided surprise would constitute his only real advantage. To blast through the steel loading-dock doors would require a charge sufficient to destroy half the building. Thus all that mattered now was surprise, and that, in turn, meant speed.

The front door thirty yards to their left was the only entrance. But it would be unlocked, leading straight into the reception area. Gray entered first, spraying forty flechettes before his eyes could even fully adjust to the blackness.

With these first four bursts, two guards fell, the first clutching his throat, another who had been seated hurled back from a desk. Then came the third kill, as a darkened figure rose from a computer console, simultaneously reaching for his Colt-Tiger pistol and screaming "I've got an intrusion here!" While a split second later, Maggie Sharp squeezed off two more flechettes that opened up his stomach and left the plaster behind him smeared with more than just blood.

Silence, while Gray lowered his left arm and those behind him hunkered into the shadows. The interior may have once been some sort of athletic court, with a staircase rising into blackness and half a dozen doors leading to offices.

Someone, possibly Cobb, said, "This is a pressure system, which means that it's going off any second now."

Although actually nearly a full minute passed before alarms began shrieking.

There were footsteps on the staircase now: at least a dozen pairs of rubber-soled shoes and what might have been the sliding bolt of an over-under conversion. Yet by this point, the intruders had already formed a phalanx, facing outward, covering all the doors and the stairs. And as those doors flung open, four grenade launchers and another eight or nine fully controlled bursts of M-90 flechettes began the fast process of decimation.

Gray counted to three before hurling the first incendiary grenade in an almost casual gesture, underhanded with his face turned away. The flames leapt some fifteen feet into the air and briefly illuminated three staggering officers, while someone else began sobbing: "Oh, Jesus Fuck. Oh, sweet Jesus!"

Two more guards were shredded into clouds of flechettes, while Gray, Arbunckle, and Cobb moved off down a passage to the right. Behind them, a hoarse voice kept shouting: "Get some! Get some! Get some!" While an obviously stricken guard screamed: "Okay, okay, okay!"

Beyond the double doors at the end of the hall lay the first of four main storage areas: a vast and darkened chamber, with steel grates on the windows and what seemed to be the remnants of a basketball hoop on one wall.

Arbunckle entered first, leaning down hard on the lever bar to release the loading-dock doors, while Cobb moved to the crates. Although there were still whispers of M-90s from below, there were no longer screams.

"We got Arafat-Timies," Cobb said softly.

A thin boy with white-blond hair appeared in the rearview mirror of a slowly backing van. When the van drew to a stop, he slid out from behind the wheel and leapt onto the loading platform.

Somewhere beyond the walls, a clearly terrified voice had started screaming: "Where the hell is everybody! Where? Where?"

But no one in that darkened room paid any attention. They continued the loading—two to lift those shoulder launchers, another perched on the floor of the van, Maggie Sharp poised at the door with that modified M-90.

"This," Cobb whispered, tapping a crate marked Ordnance Only. "And this and definitely this."

But by now Gray had already glanced at his watch, had already caught what might have been the distant whine of sirens. Then softly, but firmly: "Okay, that's it."

They emerged in stages: the kid named Jamie sliding back behind the wheel, while Cobb joined him in the cabin; Maggie Sharp backing onto the loading platform, then into the darkened recess; Gray and Arbunckle at a low run to the first van; while four more figures sprinted down the steps.

There were last bursts, of course, and someone squeezed off another M-250 into the entrance hall. But in the end, it was very quiet again, with only the sound of those incoming sirens and the rumble of the vans.

Given that incendiary grenades tend to burn for nine minutes at close to a thousand degrees, it was only a matter of time before paper and cardboard caught, then wood, then plastic, and then pretty much everything else. Thus after twenty-nine

minutes, the flames were visible for more than a mile. . . .
Which finally brought at least a thousand faces to the tenement
windows that surrounded what had once been the Second District Figueroa Armory.

CHAPTER 18

"Eleven dead and five wounded," Wimple said to Erica Strom.

Initially, the only dead Strom actually saw were the first three: two sprawled along the charred staircase and another balled up beneath a splintered desk. Then, slowly inching her gaze across the scorched linoleum, she saw the remains of at least two more: the blackened, oddly childlike forms of guards who had taken the worst of an incendiary grenade.

In all, Wimple had spent more than two hours prowling through the corridors before Strom had stalked in. White fire-suppressant covering lay in inch-deep pools, and there was the sickening stench of burned flesh and wood saturated in water.

Strom swung her head from side to side, angrily taking it all in. She looked as if she had just gotten out of bed, Wimple thought unkindly. Her hair was tousled and her lipstick carelessly slopped over her lips. In her fury, her face looked even more hideous than usual, the purple deeper, the scars more pronounced, like a relief map of emotion.

"The way we figure it, there must have been about a dozen of them," Wimple said. "Probably a lead fire team coming in over here." Then pointing to the staircase above a blown doorway: "Probably three or four more up there."

"How'd they get in?"

Wimple shook his head. "Picked up one of the compound vehicles a block or so from here, then just drove."

Fire officials in flamesuits moved purposefully through milling cops, while six or seven Trans Global employees inputted on handheld computers.

From an office at the top of the staircase, someone said, "Oh my god." Then came the sounds of retching.

"Do we have any idea what they took?" Strom snapped finally at the detective.

Wimple shrugged. "Choice collection of arms, ammunition, and supplies. They're still working up the list."

"And what about the shoulder launchers?"

"Yeah, they have the shoulder launchers. Also at least a crate or two of heart honers, which means that we'll probably have to file a national alert."

Strom gave the man an uneasy glance. "Why don't you leave that up to me, Detective?"

A twenty-one-year-old trauma analyst named Hubert appeared, a slightly lame and pale figure. Wimple had long sensed the boy was rather less the Corporate player than he let on. He was also fairly certain that the kid knew that Wimple knew, but thus far they had only exchanged glances.

"We've got a preliminary afteraction, ma'am, if you want to hear it."

Strom responded with a weary smirk. "Do I look like I don't want to hear it?"

The boy took a deep breath. "Okay, we can definitely say that there were at least a dozen and that they were mainly armed with modified 90s and gas operates. Not to mention, of course, the hot stuff."

"What about voice prints?" Wimple asked.

Hubert shook his head. "Everything electronic was knocked out before they even entered. Probably with some pretty sophisticated antitransmission system."

"And the camera?"

"Also took it out."

"Which leaves us where?" Strom hissed, turning to face both Wimple and the kid.

Wimple lumped up his mouth for a hard frown. "Well, we're obviously talking about Whistler action, if that's what you mean, ma'am. But beyond that, I'm not sure what to say."

Strom took another hard breath. "All right, then how about we just take it from the top. What we've got here is a highly organized, highly professional force. But no IDs. Is there anything of substance that can be said beyond that?"

Wimple shrugged, after a fast glance at Hubert. "The only ones who got close enough to see them can't say too much, being dead. So about the only other thing we know is that there was a black man and a woman among them. They all wore dark clothes, maybe military uniforms. No other descriptions."

"How soon was the alarm given?"

"Immediately after they left."

"Well, that would be because of the antitrans," Hubert put it.

"And then?" Strom persisted.

"The TRU-ships were up in the air in seven minutes," Wimple continued. "But they didn't even get a trace of either van, much less anything armored."

Strom took another long, hard breath. Then softly, hardly above a whisper: "And what are you doing about a door-to-door, warehouses in the area, that sort of thing?"

"It's already under way," Wimple said mildly.

Then once more, still very softly: "Jesus, do you have any idea what this is going to look like?"

But in response, all Wimple could think of saying was: "What do you say, Hub? You think maybe those inventory lists are complete now?"

Hubert nodded. "Should be, yeah. Warehouse down that hall. I don't think you'll miss it," he said.

They moved in single file, picking their way past fragments of blown plaster, glass, wood, plastic. And then, inevitably, a charred hand and wrist. Although Strom may have seen the thing, she simply kept moving.

A dozen figures in white plastic overalls were milling around the debris at the end of the corridor: some checking boxes and entering numbers into their handheld computers, others merely gazing off into nothing.

"Who's got the list?" Strom asked from the doorway.

A lean woman named Vera Shore extended one of the handhelds, while a young man named Wallace carried it to Strom. Tall, thin, with prematurely balding hair and rounded shoulders, Wallace grimaced. "We have a prelim printout, but we're doing a double check now."

"Let's see it." Strom held out her hand.

"It may not be accurate," he protested.

"Just give me the fucking printout."

Wallace blanched, then withdrew two perforated sheets of paper from his overalls. "Here," he said, holding it out. His hand was shaking.

Strom grabbed it and began to read, while Wimple moved beside her and peered down at the sheets.

Strom read aloud to herself. "Grenades, sniper systems, anti-armor missiles, Arafat-Timex missiles, ammunition. Fucking disaster!"

"Salt tablets," Wimple murmured.

"What?" she said curtly.

He pointed to the bottom of the page. "Knapsacks, canteens, salt tablets. Strange things to take."

"Who gives a fuck!" She snarled. "They got enough god-damn firepower to blow up the Towers again, and you're talking about fucking salt tablets?"

"It just seems odd," Wimple said.

"Odd!" She snorted. She whacked the sheet of paper with the back of her other hand. "Do you see this? They got Pentel-Minos grenade launchers. State-of-the-art stuff. They knew exactly what they were looking for."

"Seems that way," Wimple agreed.

"I want that Task Force on the streets. I want them up and out of bed and out there," Strom said. "I want them to start pulling people in and taking them down to the basement. I want everyone who's been questioned before back for a second round. And I want to see a whole lot of new faces. You get on the phone right now and get that happening. Understand?"

"Yes, ma'am," Wimple said.

As he walked away, skirting around a fallen ceiling beam, he congratulated himself for shutting his mouth. He'd almost said it, almost found it too difficult to resist, and it would not have been a good idea.

He'd almost said, "Good thing we have the Whistlers on the run, isn't it, Miss Strom?"

CHAPTER 19

H ank Tull the Second, Warden of the Mojave Correctional Facility, thrived on recalcitrant inmates. They gave him the chance to play with his favorite toys, to experience the true meaning of job satisfaction.

Sitting out here in the middle of the California desert, hours from civilization, his only company illiterate guards and half-dead inmates, his life tended toward tedium at times. Even he admitted it during his increasingly frequent moody periods. The few consolations available to him were thus eagerly grasped.

His very, very favorite toy was the electro-inducer, a holdover from something once called electro-convulsive therapy.

Tull was not an ignorant man. His personal library at Mojave was probably one of the best in the nation, filled with books from the previous century—many of them unavailable or banned. They lined the walls and filled cardboard boxes on the floor. Although largely self-educated, he was an astute observer of history.

His specialty, in fact, was tracing the development of modern psychiatric techniques, and he knew from his readings that their genus lay far back in the twentieth century. Strictly speaking, the antecedents flowered even earlier, toward the end of the nineteenth, particularly in the person of one Wilhelm Wundt, who established the world's first laboratory of experimental psychology at Leipzig University in Germany. From there, his disciples spread to the academic corridors of the

Western world, sponsored in large part by wealthy banking dynasties to whom their message appealed.

In a very real sense, Tull knew, the Corporate world of today owed its very existence to these early pioneers. If the groundwork had not been so well laid, the world would have been a quite different place.

Take, for example, the field of education. The first Wundt student to return home to the U.S. was G. Stanley Hall, who became president of Clark University in 1889 and played a leading role in founding the American Psychological Association—an organization that grew increasingly powerful and influential. Hall was mentor to one John Dewey of the University of Chicago and later of Columbia University. The full impact of Wundt could be appreciated when one learned that Dewey became known as the "Father of American Education."

The experimental psychologists redefined the meaning and purpose of education in a remarkably short period of time. Where once it had meant drawing out a person's innate talents by imparting knowledge of certain subjects and disciplines, it became instead the feeding of experiential data to a young brain and nervous system to get desired reactions. The teacher was no longer an educator but a guide in the socialization of the child.

The success of this system was proven by the statistics. At the beginning of the twentieth century, America had been well on the way to eradicating illiteracy. Toward the end of the century, the country had more than 40 million illiterates, and in literacy rate ranked among the world's nations in forty-fourth position, right alongside Nigeria. A few short years later, by the actual end of the century, they were fifty-second.

But that was only one facet of Wundt's influence. Hank Tull understood his true achievement, which was to rid the world of outmoded religious superstition. There was no such thing as a soul, Wundt proclaimed. Man was a stimulus-response animal—here today and gone tomorrow—with the emphasis on *animal*.

Ah, the doors that opened. One of the first rulers to take advantage of that was a fellow named Bismarck, who eagerly turned the cream of his nation's youth into cannon fodder. Why not? They wouldn't return to haunt him. As man was like any other animal, all that remained would be dust.

This belief also gave rise to many fruitful schools of psychology and psychiatry. The power of science was unleashed, without the hindrances of conscience. The innovators began to hack and slice and burn in their dedicated search for knowledge about this animal's brain. And governments were quick to utilize the skills of these practitioners. All governments, no matter what their political leanings. Torture, which had once consisted of placing people on racks and splitting them in two, became increasingly refined. And as a direct result of Wundt's early work, a new word entered the vocabulary of society: brainwashing.

The century was dotted with laudable names: Pavlov the Russian, Skinner the famous behavioral psychologist, "Jolly" West, who helped the American government conduct experiments on an unsuspecting populace with the early forerunners of today's mind-altering drugs, and many more—all supplied with funding by those who knew the true meaning of power.

Funnily enough, though, and even Hank Tull the Second thought it funny in view of the awesome drugs that had been developed this century to turn people into vegetables, his very favorite method of torture was the electro-shock applicator. Antiquated by today's standards, primitive even, it yet pleased him on a number of counts.

One of the more amusing facets was his knowledge that it had once been called a "therapy." In fact, in the previous century an entire school of psychiatrists had sworn by its efficacy, in spite of the obvious results—and they had managed to practice their experimentation for many years without hindrance.

But it was those results that really pleased him. His father had allowed him to witness its application before he even reached his teens, but he had never grown tired of seeing them.

There was nothing quite like seeing the terror in an inmate's eyes when the electrodes were attached to his body. And there was certainly nothing at all like that first jolt, when the inmate's eyes rolled back unseeingly in his head and his body grew as stiff as a board, and then went into spasms and finally uncontrollable convulsions, before lapsing into an exhausted stillness. Nothing like it. It was an almost godlike feeling to have that much power over another.

• • •

Tull sat in the glass-walled watching room while the camp psychiatrist, Dr. Lilith Palmer, strapped her patient into the electro-shock machine. From his studies, he knew that originally the EST was little more than a crude helmet fitted with electrodes—really quite primitive. Thus, although Mojave was by no means high on the requisition lists, he had made it his first point of command to wangle a rather more modern device: the Schick 1220, of which he was justly proud.

The administration platform, upon which the inmate lay, was a soft polycarbon, dotted with suction cups, each of which was centered with an electrode. The beauty of it was that no matter what the shape of the inmate's body, the surface changed contours to accommodate. Moreover, the operator could adjust not only which electrodes were active but differing degrees of charge to any particular part of the body.

The back of the head fitted into a belllike, clear plastic cover, in which another display of electrodes had been fixed. The adjustable sensitivity was excellent, ranging from an threatening tingle to a jolt that would all but turn one into toast.

The subject in this case was a male inmate, age twenty-seven, from Hut Number Three, a suspect in the recent murder of a guard. He was a small and thin man, with yellowing skin and very bad teeth. He was also at this moment very afraid.

Tull had questioned him, of course, but the man claimed to know nothing, maintaining a surly denial. It was quite likely he did know nothing, Tull suspected, but it was also too good an opportunity to pass up. It was two weeks since the machine had been utilized.

"Listen, I don't know nothing about it," the man was protesting as Lilith strapped him down.

"Hush," she said gently. "It's going to be just fine."

A comment that brought a smile to Tull's thick lips. He adored Lilith. Just under thirty years old, she was a tall and utterly gorgeous blonde, long legged, high breasted, with a sensuous mouth and the kindest blue eyes you could ever want to look down upon you. Her forté was her bedside manner: solicitous, gentle, and entirely tongue in cheek.

He knew exactly what her next comment would be, and he wasn't disappointed.

Leaning down to the terrified inmate, her beautiful face only inches from his, she said in a voice just above a whisper: "You mustn't worry. I know exactly what I'm doing, all right? I'm very highly trained, you know. So let me tell you what this is all about, all right?

"The bad news is that the pain is going to be totally unbearable. The good news is that you won't remember a thing about it. Okay, honey?"

The man began to whimper.

She lifted her gaze from the subject's body to briefly meet Tull's eyes. Her mouth broadened into a smile, and she gave him a small nod.

In response, Tull returned the smile, returned the nod, then couldn't help shifting his legs to relieve the pressure in his groin. . . . All the while Lilith, too, slowly succumbed to the sexual trance that only these moments could inspire. Indeed, it was a given that, immediately following a session, he would be the fortunate recipient of her lust—the reward, they had once joked, for allowing her to play with his toys. These were the only times they had sex together, but they were memorable. She was insatiable, energetic, and quite depraved.

"Are you sure you wouldn't like to say anything to Warden Tull before I begin?" she cooed softly to the terrified subject below her.

"Anything—I'll say anything he wants to hear, for Chrissakes! Just let me out of here," the man said.

"Oh, dear," she pouted. "I don't think he wants to hear 'anything.' I think he had some very specific questions, if you know what I mean."

"Look, wait a minute. Give me a break, okay? I know who killed Blackjack," the man said quickly. "It was one of the guards. I know, I saw him do it. I saw him. Big fella. I saw him, I swear."

She looked over at Tull and raised an eyebrow. He shook his head and sighed.

Last-minute confessions were really quite a bore. He'd heard them too often. The inmates would say anything, tell any lie, to put off their unavoidable fate. A couple of times initially he had stopped the proceedings and paid attention to it, all to no avail. He knew now when they were lying, and this young man was certainly lying through his rotting teeth.

Lilith continued her work, adjusting the setting, while her subject resumed whimpering, saliva running down his chin to his neck.

Tull, a large, corpulent man with a double chin, leaned forward in his chair, eyes now fixed on the tableau.

Lilith started to hum to herself, a signal that the proceedings were about to begin.

Then she flicked a switch.

The man gave a very slight twitch, looked surprised.

"There, how did that feel?" Lilith asked.

"A—just a little tingle," he said. And relief oozed in his voice.

"Very good," she said.

Then she extended her left hand and gave a control dial a savage twist.

The man's body contorted, his screams died in his throat, his eyes bulged, and then his limbs began to jerk uncontrollably. Like a puppet.

Tull licked his dry lips. This was what it would be like to be god. There was nothing better.

CHAPTER 20

O ver the next two days, Annie watched the stranger whenever she could—which was not that often. She saw him only in the print shop, and then only in passing, generally on the edge of her vision, like a half-glimpsed wraith. He was a model inmate in the shop, stoically following orders and efficiently doing his job. His expression remained unreadable and, as far as she could see, he spoke to no one. He never looked at her.

And yet, on some deep level, she knew that, while it appeared nothing was changing, nothing would happen any different from the way it had the day, the week, the month before; it was only time passing.

Whatever was going to happen would indeed happen. In a sense, it already had. It was simply waiting there for time and her phantom man to catch up with it. When time brought him to that particular circumstance, that moment, he would bring it to life so that everyone would see it and believe in it.

She already believed in it.

Marcie thought Annie was becoming strange and she talked to her about it.

"Listen, Annie, everyone here is crazy. You know that," she explained, her voice very calm, even a little condescending, which was unusual for her. "A little crazy or a lot, but everyone is crazy."

They were sitting in Marcie's room. It was evening, an hour before the lights-out signal. Marcie's radio was playing a Corporate marching song softly in the background.

Annie looked at her friend and saw the worry swirling around her face. In her mind's eye the swirls were purple with concern.

As she had been for days now, Annie was electrified, her nerves sticking up like pins. Sharp.

She had told Marcie nothing more. Had not specifically mentioned her phantom. He was her secret, and she would not betray it.

"It's the camp," Marcie continued. "They designed it that way. The malnutrition, the midnight inspections, the endless work, the anger of the guards . . . it's all designed to make us a little crazy, to keep us off balance, to control us."

Annie just looked at her. Not even with interest. She just looked.

"What's going on with you?" Marcie asked, her voice rising in exasperation now. "You're getting weird on me. It's like you're walking around in a glass booth, cut off from everyone, from me, separated." Her mouth twisted and her voice climbed even higher. "What's happening to you?"

Annie saw it all then. It wasn't a sudden flash of clarity—more like a calm and encompassing knowing. Marcie was afraid because she had allowed herself to love her. Not the love some women had for each other in the camp but the love of a big sister for her small one. The sister Marcie had never had; maybe even the child she had never had.

Annie supposed that she was one of the few people who had heard the story of Marcie's life, such as it was, before Mojave. Her father disappearing when she was seven. A Corporate casualty, perhaps, one of the Disappeared, or simply a victim of the increasingly dangerous streets. Her mother shooting up Methbadine, one of the then-new designer drugs, sleeping with anyone and everyone in order to get her next fix. And how at sixteen, Marcie had started turning tricks herself, mainly because there was nothing to eat at home, no clothes to wear, a landlord who said "You and your mother are going to be out on the street before you know it. I ain't running no charity here." Her mother couldn't be counted on for anything. Nothing.

Marcie's first trick had been with the landlord, a blubbery, fifty-four-year-old Iranian who became more certain than ever that he had found the land of opportunity. From then on it was easy, although she was, she assured Annie, discriminating. "After that disgusting piece of lard, I picked and chose. Young, good-looking guys with more money than brains. Guys from the hills where all the girls dressed pretty and crossed their legs, down in the tenements, looking for a good time. No strings, no feelings, you know what I mean?"

Until her mistake, which was refusing to play kinky games with an IRS agent. "And here I am." No mother ("She's dead by now."), no father ("Who knows?"), and no other family. "Just me, which is how it always was, anyway." And in the same breath: "So, don't count on no one, kid, not even me. Sure, I like ya, and we hang together, but don't count on no one, okay?"

Sure, okay . . . until, as Annie now realized—faint beams of moonlight drifting in through a dusty window, breeze singing through the chain-link fence—Marcie had started to count on her.

In the beginning Marcie had probably just felt sorry for her. Not a small thing, compassion—not at least in Mojave. Maybe Marcie saw herself behind Annie's frightened eyes. Whatever the case, she had befriended her, and over time the feelings had grown between them. They were friends. There was trust, in spite of Marcie's cautions. And there was dependence. A subtle thing: *I don't need anything, but be there for me, okay?*

Although now Marcie was starting to feel that Annie was no longer there, and the threat of that loss was obviously terrifying her—even though she would never admit it to anyone, including herself.

Annie had been staring at Marcie during these thoughts, she had no idea for how long. But in that time, Marcie's exasperation had deserted her and she just looked sadly at Annie and repeated, "In a glass booth."

"No," Annie whispered. "It's not like that at all. It's just . . ." She broke off, eyes suddenly bright, voice vibrant. "It's just how it is right now. So you mustn't worry about me. Really. Everything is going to be all right. I promise. I've never been more alive, never been better."

Her enthusiasm must have been contagious, because Marcie allowed a puzzled smile to creep ever so slightly over her lips. She cocked her head. "Why? What the hell are you talking about? What's happening with you?"

Annie looked at her friend and saw it wasn't yet time to tell her.

"Marcie, do you trust me?" she asked.

Marcie's head jerked upright. "What?"

"Trust me?"

"Uh," Marcie began, looking flustered for once. And then she allowed a belligerence to take over. "What kind of question is that?"

"A simple one."

"I told you, you don't trust no one in Mojave."

"But deep down you trust me." This time it wasn't a question.

Marcie met her eyes then. For a long moment they looked at each other, and whatever Marcie saw finally allowed her to speak. "Sure, kid, I trust you," she said, and the most noticeable trait in her voice was relief.

Annie nodded. "Then you must believe me. Everything is going to be all right. Soon. I told you I'd see the sign, and I have. It won't be long now."

In spite of herself—the misgivings that flitted through her mind, the Judas thoughts, the outright cynicism that had allowed a part of her to survive for so long—Marcie leaned forward on her bed. "Are you sure?"

"It won't be long," Annie repeated.

CHAPTER 21

Within a week of the stranger's arrival, a lot of things had begun to change—some barely significant, some barely noticeable, some almost meaningless.

Point of fact: The kid who worked in the print shop had fallen in love with Annie. It had come on fairly suddenly, first with nervous smiles when she happened to pass, then offers to help carry the stacks of paper, all the while fixing his puppy gaze on her, adoring and admiring, and quite inarticulate about what he was feeling.

"Hey, Annie! You okay?" he would ask with a piercing concern.

"Sure," she'd reply, as he shifted his feet, looked away and then back, unable to hold her gaze, while he informed her that he was all right, as all right as anyone could be in Mojave.

"Well, see you around," he'd finally mumble, and he'd shuffle on back through the ranks of the hot steel sorting tables.

And then he watched her.

Which Annie actually found quite annoying, because watching was what she did, and who was he to . . . But then it came to her that while he may have been watching, he certainly wasn't seeing. At least not clearly.

He wasn't seeing her, just some idealized vision of her, filtered through veils of romanticism and degrees of longing.

Later, while she was rolling heaps of newsprint to the loading docks, he stopped what he was doing and moved to help her, first making sure the guard wasn't watching him leave his post. The fact was, however, that supervision in the print shop was relatively lax, particularly since the unlamented demise of Blackjack.

"Want me to give you a hand?" he asked.

Not particularly, she wanted to say. But all that came out was a question: "Hey, David, tell me something: Did they ever find out who killed that guard?"

He shrugged, shook his head. "You mean Blackjack? Nah. They pulled a few people in, kept them in the box for a couple of days, gave them a bit of shock and questioned them, but I don't think they ever nailed anyone. Not that I heard."

"But what do you think?"

"About what?"

"About who did it?"

Although possibly flattered that she had asked his opinion, he immediately grew embarrassed because he had no answer. "I dunno. They say it could have been another guard. Who knows? Listen, whoever it was should get a medal. Blackjack deserved far worse."

They had reached the loading dock and a long view of hot sand to the outer gates, and churning clouds along the rim of distant mountains . . . which was another thing that was different since the arrival of the stranger. Now it seemed that there were always dark clouds in the sky.

"Annie," he began hesitantly.

"What?" she asked, wiping her forehead with the back of her arm.

He forced himself to look at her. "I sure do like you."

"I like you too," she said lightly.

He shook his head. "No, that's not . . . I mean, I really like you. More than 'like.' I . . . I think about you all the time. You know what I saying?"

"You should be thinking about yourself in this place," she said.

"I do, but I can't help it. I think about you too."

She forced a gentler tone. "Look, David, I think it's great what you said, but I can't think that way about you. Not now, maybe not ever."

"You can't stop the way I feel," he said hotly, his face burning.

She touched his thin arm with her hand. "I'll be your friend, David," she said quietly. "A good friend, the best you have, but just a friend. Okay?"

He smiled bravely then and said something about being thankful for that.

As they moved back into the shadows of the press room, she couldn't help thinking that the real problem was that David was just a kid, a year or two older than she was, but basically still just a kid. . . . Which, now that she thought about it, was probably what this camp did to everyone: turned you into a cringing child, with every fear of childhood pressing down hard every moment of the day.

"Tell me something else," she said softly when they reached the gloom of those drying racks.

"Sure," he said, trying to sound casual, but judging from his eyes she was certain he was frightened now.

"That new inmate? What's his name? Troy?" she asked. "What's he like?"

David shrugged. "I dunno. Keeps to himself mostly. Everyone leaves him alone, even the TSs. How come?"

She shook her head. "He just kinda looked like someone I knew, that's all," she lied.

"Is he?"

"No, just looked like it."

"Well, I'd stay away from him. I mean, he's pretty weird. Also, a lot of people are kind of scared of him. He's real quiet, real polite, but there's something about him, if you know what I mean."

"Is he in your hut?"

"Nah. He's in Number One, I think. I'm in Number Two." He stopped, looked quickly around, and said, "Annie, listen, I'm sorry. I mean, if what I said . . ."

She smiled, a fleetingly brilliant smile. "It's all right. We're friends, right?"

"Right," he said with a nod and turned to go back to his post.

She saw him then, her phantom man, and promptly forgot about David. He was leaning over boxes of printer cartridges, pushing them away to make room for new arrivals. He wasn't a large man, was slim, but she saw his strength in the knotted muscles of his back, in that grace with which he moved. A strong man.

She half expected him to turn, sensing that he knew she was looking at him. But he didn't. Refused to. Just continued doing what he was doing.

Hut Number One was visible from the west bathroom window of Annie's hut. Corrugated metal, like all of them. The closest men's quarters, in fact, to the women's section, separated by a few storage sheds and a strip of bare land, floodlit at night.

Although men and women inmates were segregated, Mojave lore suggested that there had been assignations. In one of those storage sheds, for instance. Late in the night, when guards were drowsy and dogs asleep. Hurried couplings amid boxes of supplies. Sweet words and tender feelings in a place where they had no right to exist.

For a long time, Annie remained fixed at the screen, gazing out across the black sand to Hut Number One . . . fingers curled through mesh, face against the cool steel, wondering what he was doing. Lying on his bed, hands behind his head, eyes fixed on the ceiling? Waiting? Waiting for time to catch up with him?

Behind her were the sounds of women preparing for bed. Exhausted women who fell onto their cots without bothering to remove their clothes. Cursing women who wondered at the purpose of sleep when they would awaken to face more of the same. Bleeding, battered, pained women who had lost all sense of their womanliness and become sexless objects. Insane, grief-stricken, apathetic, angry, bitter, lifeless, hopeless women who lived in an endless present.

It was different for her, only because of what she knew. Before her? Before her was the future. Only she knew it existed. Only she and, of course, her phantom man.

It was going to happen soon—the future. She knew that. She could feel it coming like a thunderstorm. Clouds gathering, moisture building, winds rising—all waiting for bolts of lightning to tear them apart so they could shed life on the barren desert sands.

That's what he was. One of those bolts of lightning. Just waiting for the clouds to get heavy enough, for the desert to get dry enough. Waiting for the sun to blink and lose its power.

• • •

She saw him the next night.

It was late, the lights long out, the moans of tortured dreams and the rustle of restless, tossing bodies the only sounds. She could not sleep—had only slept a matter of a few hours in the last few days, in fact. There was too much about to happen for sleep.

She was fixed at the window again, staring at Hut Number One, wondering what he was doing, when she saw the dark shape. It came not out of the door but from a window.

Like black mercury it slipped to the ground. It settled there for a moment, then moved into the shadows, across a patch of floodlit sand and into more shadows.

It was him. She could tell by the smooth, effortless motion of the shape.

She lost him in the shadows. Saw nothing but blackness. No movement.

For a second, like something flicking past the corner of the eye, she thought she saw a movement near the administration building but wasn't sure.

And so she waited. And watched.

Fifteen minutes later, he reappeared. Came out of the shadows into which he had sunk. Flitted across the patch of sand to the dark beside the hut and then slipped back through that window. All in one uninterrupted flow. Like a film playing smoothly backward.

When she saw him in the print shop the next day he continued to ignore her. She didn't mind that. It was part of his persona, his cover, so to speak.

She did her work as if in a dream, going through the motions, feeling no tiredness, blank even when Edna, one of the more vicious female guards, screamed at her to hurry in the lunch line.

Lunch was the usual gruel. Some kind of prepackaged soup, diluted a hundred times more than the directions called for. She didn't taste it.

Sonja, a girl a couple of years older than her from somewhere down in the South Bay, tried to talk during lunch, but Annie barely heard her words.

"Fucking Edna's going to wake up dead one day," Sonja said threateningly. "She wouldn't be the first guard to get it, and not the last to deserve it. Things can happen here. Things can happen."

Sonja had been arrested for stealing. She'd found a way to lift food at the Corporate commissary where she worked. Cans of meat, real milk, the odd carton of smokeless cigarettes. She'd been caught on camera, two frozen packets of vegetables in her bra, freezing her tits. She'd denied everything, of course, but there hadn't been much discussion. Straight to Mojave, where cold would never be a problem. Corporation law didn't bother much with warnings or probation these days, unless it was Corporate kids that got into trouble.

Sonja was one of those who looked at Annie with awe. Desperately wanted to be her friend. Annie treated her with the same unfailing politeness and kindness with which she treated everyone she came into contact with, something that Sonja almost resented, yet couldn't quite.

"I wish they'd all die," Sonja was saying, her anger shed, a surly bitterness replacing it.

"What?" Annie asked.

"God, Annie. Where are you these days?" Sonja said. "You're really out of it."

No, Annie wanted to say. I'm here in reality. You're the ones who are out of it. All of you. Living a dream. I'm the only one who's awake. Me and the phantom man.

Instead she just smiled apologetically at Sonja and said, "I'm sorry, I was just thinking of something."

She saw him again that night. Late again. The shadow moved out of the window again.

This time she didn't hesitate. Her window was slightly open, so she lifted it until it was large enough to fit through, unhooked the screen, and slipped out, legs first, bending backward, then her head, holding the frame with her hands.

A quick glance left and right for guards and then she took off after him, keeping her distance, seeing only a flash of motion ahead of her every now and then. Maybe not even seeing it, but definitely sensing it.

He crossed a strip of lighted sand, and she saw that he was carrying something in his right hand—what looked like a small black box, flat, about as long as a can of food.

He went between two small storage sheds and then dropped

to a crouch on the ground in a slightly darker area where the light did not reach.

She circled around one of the sheds so that she could see more clearly what he was doing. Then she fell to her haunches, as he was, and watched, hardly breathing, as still as a shadow.

This was it. What she had known about him all along. Whatever it was.

Placing the box on the ground in front of him, he fiddled with it and then seemed to lift something from it, something thin and silver.

It was an aerial, she realized. Like a radio antenna.

He pressed down on something, adjusted it with his fingers. There was nothing she could see happen, nothing she could hear, but thirty seconds later he pushed the aerial back down, and she could see by the sudden momentary relaxation of his body that his job had been done.

He rose and turned, looking around with a sweeping glance.

She shrank back against the building, willing her invisibility. For a moment he seemed to be looking directly at her, but then his glance moved on.

He moved his head up once toward the sky, held it there as if searching for something, and then moved back the way he had come.

She stood there, breathing deeply. It wasn't fear; it was excitement—and relief.

Yes, she knew things, and yes, she seldom doubted herself. But sometimes she couldn't help the doubt, for she was in a place that nurtured it. That was Mojave's job. To destroy all your beliefs, including those in yourself. What she had just seen was a supreme validation of her own sanity, of what she knew to be true.

She looked up as he had done, into the clear velvet sky, so filled with stars, suddenly so filled with fresh hope.

CHAPTER 22

For at least three hours, Annie remained at that bathroom window, clinging to the steel mesh, resting her weight on the rim of the bowl. The stench, of course, was almost more than one could bear, and twice there had been a pounding at the door. But having seen him once, she had no choice but to keep on waiting until he reappeared.

She had glimpsed him briefly throughout the day following that night she had seen him in the yard—walking through the print shop, intent upon what he was doing, not looking at anything else. And yet, somehow, she again had the feeling that he knew she was looking at him.

Later that same evening, she had seen Marcie, looking tired, strained, but otherwise pleased to see her. "Hey, kid, how's it going?" she asked.

Annie sank to the foot of the cot without replying. Some nondescript music played softly on the radio, and moths kept flitting around the naked light bulb. She ran a finger over the rough blanket, a better quality than those the other prisoners used, thicker. She looked over at Marcie: gray in the hair, a lined face, but hard blue eyes that had never surrendered. Then, without quite realizing why, she felt a rush of affection so intense it threatened to engulf her.

"What?" Marcie asked, observing her.

Annie shook her head.

"What?" Marcie repeated, smiling a little foolishly at the strange expression on Annie's face.

"Just be patient," Annie said finally.

Marcie gave her a look.

"You told me to believe that something would happen. It's going to happen. Just be patient."

Marcie narrowed her eyes. "There was a girl like you here once. Drifted through it all, eyes fixed on something nobody else saw. She hung herself," she finished cruelly.

Annie smiled.

Marcie grimaced, probably at what she had just said. "Why don't you tell me what this is all about?"

Annie rose from the bed. She was starting to vibrate again, gripped by that feeling of excited anticipation. "Please, just be patient," she said.

She rose to her feet, hesitating briefly for a quick glance over her shoulder, then moved back through the filthy lane between the barracks until she reached her own hut. There, after running a damp rag over her face, she threw herself down on her cot. Then for a long time she simply just lay there, eyes closed, measured breathing, waiting for the lights to go out.

When darkness came she did not move. She listened to the sounds around her: the deep ragged breathing, the muffled voices of dreams, the odd choked sob. Then, when all was quiet and still, she opened her eyes and slipped from the bed and went back to the window to continue her vigil.

It must have been about two in the morning when he finally appeared again, that pool of mercury dropping from the window to merge into the deeper shadows between the corrugated iron siding. She continued watching for another fifteen or twenty seconds, then gently yanked the wire mesh and also slipped out into the night . . . falling from the window like dust to settle in the sand.

This time he went in a different direction, heading toward the administration building.

She stayed a good fifty yards behind him, not afraid of losing sight because somehow she knew where he was at all times, just knew it.

He skirted the administration building, hesitated a moment, then slipped toward the communications building, the one with wires poking from the roof, reaching for the sky.

She stayed against the side wall of the administration building and watched from the corner. Lights fell from the windows, shafts of visibility that he somehow avoided. Like any phantom, he clung to shadows. At one point he stood just beside a window and seemed to peer in.

Then he went around the back wall and she could no longer see him.

She wanted to move forward but could not. It was too dangerous. He was probably just on the other side of the building. Although maybe he had gone on to explore farther. Maybe he was at the big warehouses at the back. Maybe he had even gone as far as the perimeter. But it was too dangerous to go on. Besides, he was probably just on the other side of the building, and if she stepped out from the shadows, he might return without so much as a footstep's warning, and then where would she be?

Two minutes passed. Three. No sign of him. Four minutes.

For the first time she didn't know where he was or what to do.

Where was he?

And then, very faintly, directly behind her, she heard the scuffling of sand.

Before she could react, before she could do more than blink her eyes, the hand came around her face to cover her mouth.

"Don't move, don't speak," the voice said softly in her ear.

He took her back to the tool sheds, still muffling her mouth, half carrying her. Although she didn't know exactly how he did it, he opened the door—one deft motion with a thin metal object—and pushed her inside.

He let go of her mouth, spinning her around to face him. Stood there, his eyes glinting.

"So?" he said.

She stared back at him in the gloom, seeing him really close for the first time.

He looked back at her with his dark, empty eyes.

"So, you're the watcher," he breathed out at last.

The words sent a chill through her body. *The watcher.*

"What?" she asked.

The white of his teeth suddenly showed. "I think you know what I'm talking about."

"You mean you've seen me?"

He nodded, but with no change of expression it was difficult to tell what he meant when he said, "Your eyes are like knives."

"I didn't mean anything by it. I just wanted to—"

"Forget it." And just as suddenly, his voice grew soft, relaxed. While her own muscles tensed, and the blood began pounding in her veins.

"What do you want with me?" he asked, his voice shattering her thoughts.

I want you to lead me to freedom.

How could she say that? All the certainty she had been feeling deserted her then. Whatever he was doing was important— that much she knew. Who was she, a dumb kid, to be following him around like some love-struck sweetheart? What did she really know? She couldn't look at him. Instead she fixed her eyes on some kind of electric spade.

"Tell me," he insisted.

And then her doubts left her, dissolved. She knew what she wanted. She wanted him to lead her to freedom. And she knew then what she had to do.

"I want to help you," she said.

There was silence then. She looked into his black eyes and saw nothing there except a mild interest.

"And what, exactly, do you think I'm doing?"

Her strength came back in a wave. It stiffened her body, added timbre to her voice. "Listen to me," she said intently. "I know who you are!"

"And who am I?" Was that amusement in his voice? It didn't matter.

She met his eyes again. And did more. Grasped his hand in hers. "You're the man who's going to open the gates," she said.

She felt him stiffen. Not just his body, his entire being.

"What do you mean?" he asked softly, his voice turning dangerous.

"You know what I mean," she said, more certain of herself than she had ever been.

"Who are you?"

"I'm Annie, and I'm your friend," she said softly.

His tension passed, and again that brief smile appeared, a flash of white in his mouth. "Annie," he said.

"How can I help you?" she asked.

He totally relaxed then, moved back and leaned against the wall and looked at her through the combination of dim moonlight and reflections from the passing searchlights.

"What do you know about me, Annie?" he asked, a gentleness in his voice.

Nothing. Everything, she wanted to say.

"You're different," she said. "I saw that on the day you arrived."

He nodded. "Yes, I remember that. Very well."

"So what can I do to help you?"

He appeared to think about it for a moment. "Do you have people here that you trust?" he asked.

"One. Marcie. And then there's a boy. Maybe."

"Tell me about them."

She described them both, ending with "Marcie's like you and me a little. I can trust her. I also trust David, but I don't know how together he is."

"Well, there'll come a time when you find out," he said. "In the meantime . . ."

"What?"

"You can be my watcher. You watch my back for me. I come out at the same time every night. And you can watch the others. I need to know if there's any change in procedure among the guards. Anything different that you notice. Can you do that for me, Annie?"

"Yeah, I can do that."

"But there might come a time when I ask you to do a lot more, you understand?"

"Yes."

He pushed himself away from the wall. "Well then, we'd better get back now."

He moved toward the door, but she put her hand on his arm. "Wait. I want to know your name. Your real name."

Turning those deep dark eyes on her, he hesitated for only a fraction of a second. "It's Danny," he said. "My name is Danny Klein."

CHAPTER 23

The face that stared back at Erica Strom from the bathroom mirror adjacent to her Trans Global office was, she had to admit, hideous: scars seemingly deeper and more pronounced, the flesh below her left eye someone's bad joke on a Halloween night. It was the stress, she told herself. No woman looked well under stress.

It had been a full hour since Jason Englund had called: a harsh call on the heels of his return from Trans Global Central in New York. "I think we'd better talk," he had said. Then by degrees, his smooth insinuations concerning the tenuousness of her position had been replaced by an agitated anger. Apparently he had also been taking heat.

On the televid screen, his face had lacked its customary smooth blandness, and when he ended his call with the words "I'm talking about firm results, Erica, and I'm talking about them now," his face had actually contorted with anger, something Strom had never seen before, and something she didn't particularly want to see again.

Nor did she really want to end up her days as a clerk in some Corporate outpost. Which is what Englund predicted would happen if she didn't resolve this little problem in the basin.

Which is why when she went back into her office she punched fiercely at the communications console on her desk and, when little Normal Feldt's face appeared on the screen, snarled two words: "In here!"

Feldt arrived in her office a moment later, peering anxiously through his thick glasses, his myopic eyes magnified.

143

Strom, who had been standing beside her desk, finally sat down and said, "What have we going for us tonight, right now?"

Feldt glanced at what must have been at least a dozen Mylor capsules scattered on the shag and dregs of cheap Jap gin in a plastic tumbler. Then, finally shaking his head: "Not much."

"What about that pair of Devos the Dooner brothers pulled in? The laser jockeys, or whatever they call themselves?"

Feldt cleared his throat. "Uh, died under questioning."

"And without a statement? Without even a goddamn statement?"

Feldt bit his lower lip, then jammed his hands in the pockets of his blazer, twin lightning bolts of the Trans Global crest neatly fixed to the left lapel. "Look, if I can be completely honest for a moment . . ."

Strom shook her head and smirked. "Sure, Normy, be honest with me. Tell me that those little pricks didn't know anything to begin with."

"That's not what I was going to say, ma'am."

"Then what?"

"I just think we need to change the tactic a little, maybe start moving a little more in sync with public taste."

"And what's that supposed to mean?"

"That maybe . . . Well, maybe we should ease off on the roundups."

She swung her chair around to face the window. The sky was streaked blood red, saturated with sulphur and at least another dozen pollutants from the factories that ringed the Los Angeles basin.

"Tell me something," she finally breathed. "Who am I talking to right now, Normy? Am I talking to little Mr. Feldt, Detective Wimple, or one of your PR Central pals? Hmmm? Who the hell am I talking to?"

He shrugged. "I'm just trying to help, ma'am."

"Sure. Sure you are." Then, suddenly whirling from the window to face him: "Look, why don't you just get the hell out of here and try to do something constructive for a change!"

She didn't watch Feldt leave. She simply turned back to that red vision of the basin skyline, thinking *Why? Why the hell isn't it working?*

Her other assignments hadn't been like this. The enemy had been visible, vulnerable. It had simply been a matter of pulling the strings, pushing the buttons, then driving the point home. But these Whistlers, she told herself—actually mouthing the name—were definitely something else. Not just invisible, but organized, with a multidivisional cell system and god only knew how many cut-outs. Then, too, they obviously understood the menial mind, understood what made the tenements tick.

Still, assuming that one could trace the links, she told herself—absently reaching for yet another Mylor—there should have been no reason in the world why one couldn't unravel the system. So what was she missing?

She didn't even need to pose the next question, which was how many of those so-called informants had actually proved of value. None. The so-called leads had been nothing but suspicions, attempts to carry out personal vendettas against neighbors or business rivals, and simple avarice.

So what's the answer? What's the secret, the proper focus? While at the same time also recalling something Englund either said or implied regarding the obvious failure of her three-pronged attack: her informant program that had attracted charlatans, the street pressure that had bagged a lot of dead no-gooders, and a television campaign that even she had to admit had turned out to be methane waste.

So the question remained: *What wasn't she doing?*

The problem with Erica Strom, Wimple thought, was that she didn't know how to think. Didn't have the patience for real police work. Her primary solution to all problems was force.

He sat in his plexiglass cubicle bleary-eyed, exhausted, but still gazing at his computer screen—a Lexicon 10,000.

He had had a real office of his own once. Come to think of it, his entire career in the LAPD after a brief early peak had been a slow, downward slide. When he'd finally made detective, his ambition for many years, a certain degree of autonomy had come with the promotion. His own office, to some extent his own hours, and not too much concern how he went about his job as long as he produced results. Which he had . . . considering.

Then, with the gradual but remorseless encroachment of Corporate power, everything had changed. The primary skill of a detective, a captain, and all grades above had become politics. Upward mobility within a bureaucracy. It was not something Wimple had been particularly adept at, which was why, when all was said and done, he was still a detective. . . . Second class, tired, sitting on the cusp of what they called the twilight years.

In all, Wimple had been fixed for three hours in front of the screen—sometimes actually concentrating, other times half dozing. The Whistler file he'd been scrolling was as vast as any useless Trans Global index: record after record of suspected Whistler activities and yet utterly barren of hard information. There were attacks on police and Corporate facilities, thefts of equipment and arms, the odd assassination, lists of suspected affiliates, speculative leaps of imagination, and more.

The pattern was clear, however. If ever the Whistlers were delivered a blow, their philosophy was not to retreat but to hit back twice as hard. Any apparent retreat was simply a regroup. These tactics, he presumed, originated in the mind of John Gray. And it was that mind he now attempted to understand. Know your enemy. Old advice and still valid.

Looking back, the assassination of the Corporate informer should have been predicted. The recent attack on the Figueroa Armory should have been predicted. Not specifically, of course, but an attack of some kind was exactly what Gray would have done in reaction to the heat on the streets.

It seemed, however, that Gray never did anything without a reason. Was resupply of his weapons capabilities the reason for the armory heist? Maybe, but Wimple suspected not. Gray needed the weapons for a specific reason, to fulfill a specific plan.

He scanned through what was known of John Gray's life, much like Erica Strom had done when she first arrived in Los Angeles. The murder of his parents, his arrest as a boy after he and an exmarine had attempted to gain access to records showing where his parents had been sent. The death of the marine and Gray's internment at the Mojave Correctional Facility. His remarkable escape from Mojave, during which he had killed a female guard. His reappearance years later in Los Angeles, a young man then, briefly working on the fringes of society and then disappearing again to create his Whistler persona, skillfully leaking it, bit by bit, into society and creating an almost mythical aura.

Wimple took a deep breath, exhaling through his teeth, then passed a hand across his forehead. The man had made very few mistakes. He wasn't afraid to use force, but he applied it with intelligence. Unlike Strom. And, Wimple admitted, not for the first time, he applied it with principle.

The problem was that he admired John Gray. The only time they had met, Wimple had been left with a driving impression: Here was a man of power and integrity. Which was more than he could say for his Corporate masters.

But, like it or not, they were adversaries. And if he admired him so much, Wimple thought caustically, he should be able to get inside the head of Mr. Gray and figure out what he was going to do next. Somewhere in this morass of data was a clue.

He punched up the inventory of what had been taken at the armory and began to read through it for the fifth or sixth time.

Weapons, weapons, weapons, and that curious anomaly of salt tablets and water canteens.

And then, in a flash of associated thought, a vision of dry salt beds and heat and endless sand, Phillip Wimple knew what John Gray's next target would be.

Wimple sat for three more hours in his plexiglass box. The sun had long gone, replaced by a fraction of a moon that was now high in the cloudless sky. For the most part he sat and remembered his only visit to Mojave, years earlier.

He'd been sent there to question two subjects about a related crime—not the one they had been sent there for, which was some kind of civil disturbance. He remembered how the place had risen out of the desert, like some kind of shimmering monster, the long low huts housing the prisoners, the brutal arrogance of the guards, and, above all, the sallow, haggard, hopeless faces of the prisoners.

Wimple had worked in the underbelly of society long enough not to be affected by it. He'd seen decapitated children, screaming addicts, slime that would have been refused entry into a sewer pipe. But nothing had shaken him as much as that day at Mojave.

He had been on the force for about twelve years then, slowly watching the mandate change from a war on criminals to a war against people forced into crime by an evolving power structure. The initial inmates at Mojave had been protesters: intellectuals, academics, politicians cut from the wrong cloth, libertarians. The outspoken whose very voices had made them criminals in a newly defined era.

Of course, his conscience had bothered him after that first visit to Mojave—more than he would have ever admitted to himself. But he had pushed it aside, claiming he had a job to do. Regardless of who was in power, one had to do what one could to make the streets safe for decent citizens—as if there were any decent citizens left.

He rose and moved to the window. TRU-ships swept past, returning from patrols. Lights flickered from the tenements below. Down there, people were doing what they had always tried to do: simply live their lives with as much dignity as they could muster. That much hadn't changed in thirty years.

What was Mojave like these days? he wondered. Probably worse—although when he was there he'd seen the interrogation rooms, and they had been bad enough. At that time they had just been constructing the crematorium back behind the main buildings. Apparently more people died there than could be conveniently buried. But it had become a forgotten, largely unsupervised place, and the Corporate hand had, if anything, grown heavier. Yes, it was probably worse.

And that was John Gray's target. He was returning back to his beginnings, probably to raze them to the ground.

Wimple turned and stared at his telephone. He should pick it up and call Strom. When she answered he should say "I've figured out the Whistlers' next target, Chief Inspector. We can be waiting there for them."

And when she asked what it was, what should he say? "Well, Miss Strom, it is an affront to so-called civilization. It is an obscenity in the desert. And John Gray is going to destroy it."

He turned away from the telephone and stared once more out the window.

CHAPTER 24

The sheer number of people involved made it difficult for authorities to control movement within Los Angeles County and its environs. People still commuted to work in the city, still clogged the city from the South Bay, the northern enclaves, San Bernardino and Riverside. The best the police and other security agencies could do was the odd spot check, plus constant surveillance through the vid monitors that lined the freeways and the boarding areas and ticket counters of the bus and railway stations.

John Gray had nineteen people, supplies, and arms to move out of Los Angeles to the desert. Of those nineteen, thirteen could be considered hard-core: trained, experienced, guerrilla fighters. The other six varied in their abilities, if not their enthusiasm, and, according to those abilities, would be assigned support functions at varying distances from the action.

The move out of the city was accomplished over a two-day period, the rendezvous point fixed outside of Victorville at the farm of a sympathizer named Don Candy. Over time, Gray had utilized Candy's generosity perhaps more sparingly than necessary, usually only when he needed a stopping-off point for someone passing out of the city and into the vast and still relatively anonymous heartland or to the East Coast.

This was an entirely different matter: nineteen people and three vehicles milling around in Candy's sheds between bales of hay and bags of fertilizer.

As planned, Gray arrived with the last load. Candy, wizened and sunburned and as thin as a rail, had met him on the doorstep. It was cold, but a cold that was clean and smelled of the high desert and surrounding mountains. Then, too, there was coffee in the kitchen, Candy said—almost the real thing.

"I thought you'd be coming," Candy said.

Gray looked at him. "Is that so?"

Candy shrugged. "Just that it's been long enough. You know?"

"Yeah. Long enough."

"And now you gone and got yourself famous, too." Candy smiled. "I mean, hell, they've even got a television program all about you and your people. Which don't say much about the truth, except that you must be driving somebody to sheer desperation."

"Yeah." Gray nodded. "Desperation." Then, suddenly lifting his gaze from the rim of the cup: "Tell me something. You seen the old man at all?"

Candy nodded. "He stopped in for a visit about six months back. Said he hadn't seen you for five years."

"Six."

"But he always asks about you."

"I think about him."

"He's real proud of you, Johnny, and that's rare these days." Candy twirled his coffee cup in his hand and looked down at it. "You heading up there?"

"Maybe," Gray said.

Candy spread his palms. "None of my business."

Gray pushed back his chair and rose. "I need to check on my people. We'll be out of here by tonight."

"Will you stop in on the way back?"

Gray shook his head. "No. They're going to be all over the valley here. We'll clean up after we leave, but you might double check."

"I'll sweep up," Candy promised.

They moved out with a darkness that was nearly complete under a dim moon. In all, there were three vans: two Nisso-Fords with *Pacific Rim Forever* stickers plastered on the bumper and a Mini-Volks with a shattered rear window. From the bisecting road, they turned north on the old 15, then moved along the desert tracks to detour around Barstow before finally sweeping back onto Interstate 40 just beyond the last checkpoint. Two hours later, Gray led them onto another desert road, heading for a mountain range.

The vans were stashed in a foothill gulch, covered with camouflage tarps and unloaded save for six crates of freeze-dried food and two boxes of medical supplies.

"They're not for us," Gray explained when Jackie Arbunckle asked. He looked at the others. "I suggest you try to get some sleep, because after this little nap that's the first thing that's going to be at a premium. Then we're going to take a hike." He pointed at the distant peaks.

Arbunckle gazed out apprehensively at the desolate landscape—the impossibly long stretch of scrub rising to Joshua Trees and clumps of the Lord's Candle, then higher still to the first belt of pines. Somewhere still higher, a coyote howled.

"Dis ain't de city," he said at last. "Dat much I can tell you fo sure."

"No," whispered Maggie Sharp. "This is like . . . This is like where I grew up, like home."

"Yeah, well, it ain't no home o' mine," Arbunckle grumbled.

Then for a while, they simply sat: the black man continually shifting his gaze from the empty road below to the highway beyond, the others dozing beneath black thermal blankets, while Gray continued watching the trees above.

Gray was the first one awake, if indeed he had been asleep. He had closed his eyes finally, but visions of the past had paraded before him like ghosts appearing out of steaming desert winds.

His parents, the emptiness of the house after they had been taken away, his fruitless search, then the arrest and his arrival at Mojave, where he finally understood the true depravity of the Corporate system, and then . . . and then . . . and then.

The Old Wolf.

It was cold, and in a perfect world Gray would have yanked the cap of a butane burner. But the first dim rays of sunlight had already risen on the far horizon, and in this country smoke could be seen for miles. So he contented himself with a check of his weapons and, when that was done, slowly moved out across the clumps of scrub for another long look at the mountains—the mountains in which he had grown up and become a man.

Where the Old Wolf waited. He had spotted them already. Gray was sure of that. As they began the long ascent, weighed down by some fifty pounds of polycarbonate, stainless steel, and compressed gas flechettes, he would definitely be looking down at them, wondering what Johnny was up to now. Or perhaps he'd already guessed.

"So you feel it too, huh?"

Gray turned slowly to his left and into the eyes of the twelve-year-old Paolo. Earlier, he had been undecided as to whether or not the boy was needed, but in the end there was no denying his very real sense of what lay beyond anyone's sight.

"Yeah," Gray breathed. "I feel it too."

"So he's pretty strong, huh? I mean he's really something, huh?"

"Yeah. He's really something."

"But a friend, right?"

"Yeah, he's a friend."

The boy sank to his haunches, jabbing a stick in what might have been a rodent's hole. "So how come you keep thinking about him? You worried that maybe he's not going to be glad to see you? Or is it something else?"

Gray looked at the boy but finally only shrugged. "Yeah, it's something else," he said. Then, rising to his feet, he nodded to the others to start moving.

For the first hour or so, he mainly kept his thoughts on the practical matters: on the fact that TRU-ships were still known to patrol these hills, on the fact that in the late 2020s one of the National Guard posts had supposedly scattered the high ground with jelly mines, on the fact that Arbunckle was definitely on edge while Maggie Sharp was a little too taken with the scenery. Then by degrees, and without even noticing, his thoughts returned to the Wolf.

Because how could you ever forget what it had been like to live with that man at fourteen years old after everything had fallen to pieces? Life, family, home—all gone? And then to sit with the man in the evenings while he talked about the moves and the countermoves, the fast strikes and the slow attrition? To squeeze the trigger of your first M-90 while he whispered from a rotting log: *Let it squeeze itself?* To watch him move through the darkness like a breath of wind, or mold a fist full of plastique into the exhaust pipe of an old Nissan-Climax.

And then how could you ever forget what he had said about command?

"Give people something to believe in and let them know you'll lead them to it, and they'll do anything for you. The goal has to be greater than you are, greater than they are. If you believe in it, they will too, and if you demonstrate that you're willing to sacrifice anything for that goal they'll follow you to the ends of the earth."

One word of wisdom among many.

"If they hit you, you hit them back twice as hard. Always. You never let the enemy know that he hurt you. Make him think that his hardest blow was nothing, that all he did was inspire you to fight back even harder.

"Every enemy has something they overlook. Something that they think is impregnable. Nothing is impregnable. In fact, the things they think impregnable are the ones that are most vulnerable, just for that very reason."

And the hardest one: "Above all, you've got to be filled with righteousness, Johnny. You can never doubt yourself or the rightness of your mission. And if you ever do, never show your men. Never."

Most important, the Old Wolf taught what he called the Way of the Warrior, something Gray learned was actually a state of mind, a way of being. And slowly, through all of this, so gradually he didn't even really notice the progression, the hate he had felt at the camp and during the weeks after his escape was washed away, replaced by a calm and unshakable resolve.

William Alison Wolfe watched his protegé and nineteen others make their way slowly up the mountain. He sat in a cleft between two giant rocks, humming quietly to himself and every now and then lifting the binoculars to his eyes to check their progress.

He wore his usual uniform: self-made buckskin trousers and shirt, tire-tread boots, and a tattered black beret. Long white hair fell to his shoulders. A long-bladed knife of ancient design hung from his belt, and an old, heavy-barreled sniper-system rifle leaned against the rock beside him.

Just behind him, pink tongue lolling out, was Patton, his real wolf, or at least what was left of the breed, raised since an abandoned cub.

"Lookin' good, Johnny. Lookin' good," he murmured.

It was slow going for them, he saw. They were weighed down with weaponry and ammunition, some of it state-of-the-art stuff he'd heard of and never seen.

They had, he thought with a grim smile, just about enough firepower there to take Mojave.

"How much higher we go?" Arbunckle sighed. The Jamaican was breathing heavily, his feet slipping on dry pine needles.

Gray turned his head, a brief flicker of amusement in his eyes. "Mojave is on the other side of these mountains." He paused, then took pity on him. "We don't have to go to the very top. There's a pass through. We'll be stopping near there for the night."

He took a breath and looked back at the others. They all seemed to be doing okay, except maybe for Bill Casey. He was a communications genius, not a field person. Older than most of them, he was more likely to tire. The heavy pack on his back contained a powerful radio-jamming device and their own long-range signal equipment. In addition, each person had short-range radios in their belts.

Gray, Arbunckle noticed, seemed completely at home in this terrain, walking surefootedly along the deer paths they were taking, apparently not even looking around for landmarks but forging straight ahead. Nor was he even breathing heavily.

He wondered idly where Danny Klein was. Gray hadn't said and nobody had asked. They knew better by now. Gray told them what they needed to know when they needed to know it. It was better that way. They all trusted him.

Jackie had followed John Gray for two years now. He'd started out as a musician in New York, but there wasn't much call for musicians in this Corporate world. Then he'd done a stint in the army for four years, moving into a position as a computer technician after the first two years, when the belated aptitude tests showed that was where he belonged. When he got out he stayed in the computer field, working for the Man back in his hometown.

Probably still be there if his father hadn't been arrested after an IRS crackdown. His father, a lab technician and a widower near retirement, had managed to save a few bucks through the years—a rare and suspicious accomplishment. The IRS, however, thought he had other assets—undeclared assets.

Jackie had tried every contact he had to get him released, but it hadn't helped. The best he'd managed was a ten-minute visit to his father, and it was ten minutes that changed his life. The old man had been questioned about his "hidden assets," and his face was bruised, his arm broken. He had asked his son what the world had come to.

Jackie forsook the legal channels then. Instead he electronically gatecrashed the IRS computer system and put in a requisition order for his father's release. As soon as they let him out the gate, Jackie got him out of town, sending him down to Miami and then on board the boat of an old army friend who ran him over to Jamaica. Then, knowing his activities would be traced, Jackie disappeared into the tenements himself, finally making his way out west to Los Angeles, where there was a woman he knew from his musician days.

He made his living producing illegal computer programs that circumvented the Corporate systems. "Making some changes," he told people. In certain less than desirable circles he gained quite a reputation. It was only a matter of time before John Gray found him and said, "Do you want to make some real changes?"

And so he had. Indeed. Here he was, a New York boy out in the wilds, short of breath, trudging up a mountain to meet a phantom called the Wolf.

Even the others seemed to sense the Old Wolf at least a full minute before he actually appeared. Maggie Sharp had paused just inside the shadows of the pines, Paolo Cruz drawing up beside her, while Arbunckle remained a pace or two behind. Someone, possibly Casey, had said, "What the fuck is going on?"

But no one bothered to respond, because by then Gray had stepped ahead into a mottled clearing and stopped.

"Hello, Johnny," the old man said softly.

At which point Gray nodded, took another step or two, then paused in front of the stock-still figure: long white hair past his shoulders, some sort of ancient M-16 in his left hand, while the right hand rested on the head of a mangy canine. As thin as a rail, the man could have been a hundred years old. Lined face, but with bright, blue-green eyes that looked like a boy's.

"It's good to see you," Gray finally breathed.

"It's good to see you too," the old man replied.

Then for a long time, they simply remained facing one another . . . unsmiling, unmoving, barely even breathing.

"So this is what you got, huh?" the old man finally said, shifting his eyes to the others.

"Some of them."

"Heard 'em a long way away. Hell, smelled 'em before that."

Gray nodded. "Yeah, well, they're not used to the country."

"Fair enough," and he turned on his heels to take the lead, the dog loping beside him.

CHAPTER 25

Nothing much had changed since Gray had last been here. The mountains were eternal and tended to stay the same—as did the Old Wolf's home, a cave set in a cliff with a commanding view of all approaches.

Then, too, there were all those minor objects evoking memories: the deerskin hammocks, the dining table welded from the chassis of a '97 Ford, the methane stove, squirrel-fat lanterns, the chandelier made from the antlers of a big buck, and, of course, in the back of the cave, the arsenal of weapons.

As for the Old Wolf, there were times when Gray thought of him as being eternal as well. True, his face bore deeper lines and his step seemed a little slower, but even decades earlier, he had looked a hundred years old. If anything, his eyes were now even brighter, with a deeper sense of serenity, an acceptance of things that might not change for at least another hundred years or so.

The fire was lighted just after darkness fell, and from a cove of rocks came a freshly slaughtered deer. The carcass was then placed on a spit of automobile rods—probably from that same '97 Ford. This was not only real, unadulterated by soy, meat, something many of the group had never tasted, but venison—something none of them except Gray and, perhaps, Maggie Sharp had ever tasted.

While the others sat around the fire, drinking coffee and some kind of bathtub alcohol that Wolfe had pulled from his reserves, Gray and the old man retired deeper into the cave and faced one another from across that sheet of rusting steel.

Then again, they simply looked at one another—a silent and appreciative examination. When the Old Wolf finally broke the silence, his voice was soft, dry, very much as Gray had remembered it.

"So this is your army, huh?"

"More or less, yeah."

"What did you tell them about me?"

"Not much."

"You tell them how we met?"

"Not really."

"Well, that's about right." Then, shaking his head with an enigmatic smile: "But of course, that doesn't mean I don't need to know about them."

Gray shrugged. "There isn't a whole lot to say. The one who looks like a half-wit, name is Dobie Bloom. Majored in mathematics at MIT until his parents were killed in a Corporate raid on dissenting intellectuals. He came out West on the run and I supplied him with passes into the westside. Now he delivers groceries to the Corporate elite.

"The little bald guy in his early fifties is Alexis Vermeer. His wife was raped by LAPD goons. Killed, actually. I found him in a bad way. He was a middleman until I had to pull him out. Now he's got the opportunity to do what he wanted to do all along, which is to kill them.

"The kid—not the real young one, but the other one with the long blond hair? He's what they call a Rorrer, one of the underground music kids. But the Corps won't let him play his music, so he walks with us."

"And the others?" Wolfe asked.

Gray shrugged again. "Pretty much the same. The girl's from back east, one of the heartland losers. She can hit the head of a pin at a hundred yards with a rifle. The black guy's out of New York. The red-haired guy I picked up locally. Does the weapons." He hesitated. "Well, you're the one who originally said it, didn't you? Start with the dispossessed, the down and out. So that's what I got."

"I also told you that the only way to avoid the Corporate monster was to stop being human. Have you done that one too, Johnny?"

Gray smiled, but only very faintly, while vaguely wondering where the old man got his coffee, and supposed that he must still have links to the city. But all he finally said was: "Well,

I don't take prisoners, if that's what you mean."

Wolfe rose from his automotive table and moved to a make-shift cupboard suspended from the granite by tendrils of chicken wire. Among the collection of preserved bottles were at least two more canisters of whiskey: pale, harsh, but better than nothing.

"Did I tell you I've been salvaging myself?" he said at last. "Digging down to the core. Taking the Way of the Warrior to its logical conclusion."

Gray looked at him, still thinking about the coffee, about who else and what else the old man might have going for him.

"I guess you could call it a stripping process," Wolfe continued, "taking all the nonessentials away. Getting down to the mother lode."

"So what's the point?"

The old man took a hard swig of the whiskey, then laid the bottle on the table. "No point . . . except that if you're thinking of hitting Mojave out of revenge, then you'd better think again. 'Cause revenge is not what this war is all about, Johnny. The moment you start thinking revenge, you stop thinking clearly. And the moment you stop thinking clearly, you're dead."

"So what do you do about a guy like Warden Tull? What do you do when you're facing a son of a bitch like that?"

Wolfe ran his sleeve across his mouth. "Oh, you kill him," he said. "But you do it with a mind that is absolutely clear."

They ate in relative silence: Gray and the old man in one corner of the darkness, the others somewhat closer to the cave's mouth. Once or twice Arbunckle whispered to Maggie Sharp, and Sharp in turn exchanged glances with Bloom. But otherwise it seemed that no one had much of anything to say.

Still, later, when the others had fallen asleep, Gray returned to the blacker ends of the cave with the Wolf and began to talk about some of the more recent runs: the hit on that armory, the hit on the informants, the night that Danny Klein did the IRS. He spoke without being prompted, describing events without reference to precise times or places. When he talked about Strom, however, he couldn't seem to keep himself from describing the bitch's face.

In response, the old man shut his eyes for a moment, for at least five seconds, as if trying to summon one clear vision of her. Then he nodded and said, "I've met a thousand like her. Killing machines. You wind them up and point them, and they go to work till you either do them in or they rot in their own pus."

"Yeah, well, this one's going to rot for a long time before the clock stops ticking," Gray breathed.

"So end it. Take her out on the fly."

Gray took another long pull on one of the old man's hand-rolls. "Oh, I've thought about it. But where does it get you? They'd just unearth another one." Then, glancing up with the ghost of smile: "Besides, I'm not sure I could do it with a clean mind. Not tonight, anyway."

Wolfe rose to his feet, moved to that cupboard, and poured himself another cup of his dreadful booze.

"No," he said softly. "You missed the point. I'm not saying you don't act. I'm just saying you got to move beyond the emotion. Now, in this particular case, I'd probably agree with you. See, 'cause right now you're the one acting. All they can do now is react, which means that you have the power, not them. And while you're growing, they're contracting, because nothing can stay the same size for any long period of time. You either grow or contract. Do you understand?"

When Gray looked silently back at him, the Old Wolf smiled. "You think that's just words, don't you. But it's not. Didn't just make it up, son. It's natural law, as immutable as the sun's rising every day."

"Yeah, well, there's only so many days we can wait, old man."

"Of course, there's only so many days. So when you going down?"

"Tomorrow night I make the delivery to my man inside. If all goes well, then we hit them on Thursday night when there's no moon."

The Old Wolf nodded approvingly. "You know, if I was younger, even five or ten years . . ."

Gray looked at him again. "So why don't you?"

The old man wet his lips, gazing into the last of the fire. Then, finally shaking his head: "Hell, I'd only slow you down."

CHAPTER 26

It was late Tuesday night when Annie Fumito once more followed Klein into the shadows. To begin with, she moved slowly, easing the screen from the women's latrine, then inching her shoulders through the fiberboard window. Although it was not particularly cold, she could not seem to keep from shivering, and the blackness was almost palpable. Before moving off, she was careful to replace the screen, so that when she returned her fingers would at least find an inch or two.

She waited until the count of seven before leaving the deeper shadows, counting the sweep of the floodlights and then moving at a half crouch to the edge of the marshaling yard, when Klein was waiting.

He wore blue jeans and a cotton jersey, and although nothing seemed physically different about him, she definitely sensed the tension: a cat, not quite but almost, ready to spring.

"Okay, Annie, this is how we play it," he said softly. "In twenty seconds, I'm going out to the perimeter. Out there. All you got to do is stay here and watch my back. You see anything, you hear anything, you sense anything, you use this."

He handed her what looked like an old fountain pen, but with a button on the end instead of a nib. "I got one just like it, and once you activate it by pressing this button, I'll know. Now, you got any questions?"

She hesitated, looked at him, then simply said it: "What happens if you don't come back?"

He may have smiled, but again it was hard to tell. "I always come back, honey."

Then, just as suddenly as he had appeared, he was gone . . . melting back out into the blackness, with only the faintest whisper of a footstep.

Three, maybe four minutes later, she briefly thought she saw him skirting the far perimeter just outside the death strip. But then again, it may have only been the play of shadows from the tumbleweed or a desert hawk skimming over the sand in search of its prey.

In all, Klein had spent four days timing the Mojave security routines: the sweep of the searchlights, the movements of the guards and the dog patrols. Although the schedules were rigorously kept, the overall state of security was lax—an inevitable consequence of a long stretch in a place where rebellion was dead. Yes, the guards made sure there was control, but it was a lax control, a habit, a six-hour shift spent thinking about what was on the tube or that beer in the fridge. And the routine never varied.

Right now, for instance, he knew that the dogs were on the eastern perimeter, while in eight-plus minutes, the patrol leader would shuffle back to Center One for a coffee and whatever. Then comes another twenty-minute break and an easy stroll to the northern perimeter until the *Joey Boar Show* at eleven o'clock.

No less predictable were the searchlights, which were on automatic relay: circle, circle, circle. Unbelievable, but a hundred and fifty generally incompetent guards had fifteen hundred inmates in their charge, simply because they had the weapons and authority, and the inmates believed they had no recourse.

He paused sixty yards past the last storage huts, pressing himself to the ground as the east-end lights swept across the flagstones. Not that there was much to worry about, because as far as he'd been able to figure, the tower guards didn't even bother following the light with vision. They were satisfied simply that it was there.

As soon as it passed, he scrambled back up and continued his run to the perimeter.

Gray, he supposed, would be having a slightly tougher time of it, not only scrambling between the searchlights over the death zone beyond the wire, but also playing tip-toe through the mines. . . . All because some wary or bored desk jockey had decided that there was marginally more danger from the outside than from within. Which, Klein supposed, was probably true.

He paused again at the first ring of stacks marking the perimeter, then fell to his stomach again where the ground was slightly hollowed. He lay there and peered into the gloom ahead. Nothing.

The beam of light swept toward him again, and he pressed his face right into the sand, consciously thinking *I'm dirt. I'm a shadow. I'm nothing.*

Then, lifting his head again: *Where the fuck are you, Johnny boy?*

Typically, Gray appeared in stages—first as the shadow of slow-rolling tumbleweed, then as the wind through the dunes, then at last as the voiceless voice: *I'm right here. Right here.*

His face was blackened and vaguely ghostly through the triangles of chain link. In one hand he had a bag, in the other an electronic scanner, a device Cobb had developed specifically to detect the mines in the death zone. They lay on their stomachs, looking at each other.

"I think I got what you want," Gray said.

"Toss it over after the next sweep of the light," Klein replied.

Gray glanced up at the fence. Chain link, razor wire on the top, about twenty feet high, electrified, of course. Then softly, as if to himself: "I forgot how high they were."

Klein nodded, but replied only: "The light swings back in about seventy seconds."

"Tell me about the rest of the patrols."

Klein ran down the schedule, including out-of-camp patrols and a list of equipment and armor.

When he finished, Gray glanced at his wristwatch. "So everything going okay in there?"

Klein shrugged. "What do you think?"

"I mean, no particular problems?"

"Not really. Except that I had to do one of them."

"What are you talking about?"

But by this time the light was back. When it passed, they both rose and slid back four paces, and Gray began to swing the black canvas bag in his hand, getting a rhythm, increasing momentum. He let it go and watched it clear the top of the fence by a foot.

Klein took another step back and caught it in both arms. He immediately fell to his knees and crawled back to the fence.

"All right," Gray said. "We'll be here Thursday night unless I hear anything different from you."

"Sure," Klein replied. "Thursday night unless . . ." But he broke off with a soft "Shit."

"What's the matter?"

Klein withdrew that flat black fountain pen from the breast pocket of his shirt—the light now glowing red. "I think you'd better get the fuck out of here," he said.

There was a harsh shout, then the bark of a dog. Two searchlights swung back toward the shed where he had left Annie. Both men fell totally flat.

"What?" Gray said fiercely.

"I had someone watching my back. A kid. I think they may have her."

"Does she know anything?"

"Who I am. No details. But you'd better get the fuck away from here right now."

"Will she talk?"

"Maybe. Probably. Look, we got to go, man. And I mean now."

There were more shouts, a chorus of more dogs, some clearly enraged.

"Look, I got to know," Gray hissed. "You understand? We've got—"

"I'll let you know," Klein said.

Gray started to move off, then hesitated again. "If she breaks before tomorrow . . ."

"Then you'll just have to get in without my help—or cancel. Now, go. Right now, Johnny. We got to go."

Then, although Gray may have whispered something—Good luck, take care, something—all Klein finally heard was the sound of his steps, moving in a half crouch and sweeping the ground fast with his scanner, while weaving through the traps.

For two more minutes Klein continued to wait in the shadows of the chain link—two hard minutes waiting for the lights to resume their regular sweep. Whatever had happened to Annie was over.

He was tempted to remain very still until he was certain things had calmed down, but apart from the possibility of a perimeter check, there was also a concern that the guards would check the barracks. But no more lights came on. Apparently Annie was considered a sole miscreant—at least for now.

He looked in the bag Gray had given him. Twelve M-80 minigrenades with three-to-zero hour timers for extended detonation and a broken-down Steyr machine pistol with four clips taped to the barrel. Fine, he thought. Let 'em try and take me. There was also a digital watch with luminous figures.

He made his way cautiously back to where he had left her. It was probably the safest place in the camp right now. When he reached it he scanned the area quickly and found what he was looking for. Anyone else, not particularly looking, would have thought it a twig.

The radio signal he had given her was lying between two flagstones, about ten yards from where she had been sitting. Well, at least she could think.

After stashing his load under the floorboards in a tool shed— deep among cans of hardened whitewash and mounds of petrified rags—he slipped back to his barracks, silently entering through the window above the latrine. As he eased down to the filthy floorboards, he briefly thought he heard a young girl's scream from out across the marshaling yard. But then again, it may have just been the wind through loose sheets of corrugated iron.

CHAPTER 27

Warden Tull was not informed of the attempted escape until breakfast was brought to his room at eight o'clock the following morning. Then, although still wearing a mohair robe, suede slippers, and a hair net, he immediately requested the presence of his deputy.

Avery Wallace, who took care of Mojave affairs during those periods when the warden slept or was otherwise occupied with pleasures, had once been destined for Corporate stardom. Tall and thin, with features once patrician, but now displaying the ravages of debauchery, he came from one of the better Boston families with strong Corporate ties. By the time he was thirty, he had risen to a rank of deputy district director for Trans Global's Boston office, while by the age of thirty-four he had slipped to Correcto, the Trans Global subsidiary that administered all the penal institutions in the country. Although initially horrified to learn that his new post was at Mojave, after nearly seven years his horror had turned to a dull acceptance, which only occasionally rose to expressed resentment.

It was not his proclivity for young boys that had disturbed his Corporate masters, nor that he had maintained a veritable harem of them, but his habit of skimming Corporate monies from accounts in order to support these habits. Avarice and profligacy would normally be overlooked, but not when the victim was the Consortium. If it were not for his familial connections, he would have been executed. The next-best punishment was Mojave.

Tull did not like his deputy much. In particular, he resented Wallace's habit of dropping the names of Corporate luminaries into his conversations, as if they still meant something in terms of influential contacts. He did not hesitate to remind his deputy on occasion that while it might passeth all understanding, he, Henry Tull the Second, had chosen his post at Mojave, while Wallace had been banished there. Nor did he hesitate to remind Wallace that if he were no longer needed at Mojave he would not be given a more pleasant assignment. It was a workable relationship, in Tull's view.

"I don't suppose you're going to tell me about the escape?" Tull asked as soon as his deputy entered his quarters. "Or am I expected to read about in the camp circular?" He was spreading marmalade onto a piece of toast, and he waved the knife at one of the dining chairs.

Wallace sat obediently and poured himself a cup of coffee from the silver pot when Tull next waved at that. "There's not much to tell. Young girl looking for a way out. We got her in a holding cell."

Tull took a bite of toast and spoke while he chewed. "What sort of preparations?"

"Nothing, really."

"Then how the hell did she expect to get out?"

Wallace spread his hands. "I don't imagine it was an entirely rational decision. Apparently she was looking for a hole in the perimeter, or perhaps hoping to stow away in one of the trucks."

Tull looked unblinkingly at his deputy, then shook his head sadly. "And you believed that?"

Wallace looked flustered. "Well . . ."

"Anyone else involved?" Tull snapped.

"No, she was quite alone. More or less just wandering around."

"You do a bed check?"

"Well, under the circumstances . . ."

Tull shook his head again, and Wallace lapsed into silence. "I want a prisoner count, Wally, and I want it now."

Wallace stood, bumping the table and spilling coffee from his cup into the saucer. "Yes, sir."

"And I'll want to talk to her myself a little later," Tull added.

Tull sighed heavily as he watched his deputy leave the room.

The man was a moron, of course, but at least he was controllable. Moreover, he would never become a serious contender for the number-one spot . . . which, all things considered, was what counted. For Tull liked his job. Indeed, all he had ever desired was to reign as king in this little fiefdom. With the grace of god, as he often stated to his staff, he intended to die at Mojave, just as his father had before him. Not immediately, he would joke to his appreciative captive audience, but when he was old and senile.

He popped the last piece of toast into his mouth. One couldn't be too careful about attempted escapes. The powers that be didn't care how many prisoners died in Mojave—in fact, sooner or later they would all die here—the only sin was to let them escape. Maybe it was as Wallace had said: just a crazy girl wandering around, looking for a hole in the wall. Maybe not. He'd find out later in the day. In the meantime, she wasn't going anywhere.

When at one o'clock in the afternoon, his secretary informed him that Marcie wished an audience, Tull found himself more thoroughly startled than he had been in years. By any measure, it was a unique event. For Marcie was totally self-sufficient, had never asked for anything. In fact, every few months he would stop in and see her, just to make sure she didn't need anything. It was a tradition his father had started, this special view of Marcie, and he continued it, even though he didn't quite understand why.

"There's some people more valuable to you alive than dead," the old man had told him once. "She's a special one that, and as long as she don't cause no trouble, don't cause her none." That's all he had ever said about her, but the words had been endowed with an almost biblical finality, and Tull had seen fit to follow them.

It was just after two o'clock when she actually appeared, entering his office with a vaguely unsettling air of indifference, declining an offer of grapefruit juiced (canned) or orange juice (fresh). She sat without an invitation, then leveled those calm, frank blue eyes at him and said only, "A favor, Warden. If you please."

There was also something vaguely disturbing about the way she sat, stiff and slightly cocked to the left.

"Well, obviously, any reasonable request . . ."

"The kid from last night. Annie Fumito."

Tull nodded, but he couldn't quite manage to meet her gaze. "What about her?"

"I want you to go easy on her."

Tull pursed his lips. "Friend of yours?"

"Yes. She's a friend of mine."

Tull ran an idle finger along the edge of the page before him, circling the name Fumito . . . once, twice, three times. "Sometimes I think we're a lot alike, you and I. Opposite ends of the fence, so to speak, but a lot alike." He lifted his gaze but saw nothing he could recognize as either fear or hatred. "The problem is, I can't always act in accord with my feelings. I have to bear in mind the broader view . . . if you get my point."

But all the woman said was: "She's just a kid, Warden."

"Even so, an example must be made. Otherwise, where are we? Anarchy? Wholesale disregard of order? Where?"

"She wasn't trying to escape."

"That's not what the guard claims. Indeed, says here that those were the first words out of her mouth. She said herself that she intended to make a break for it."

"I don't believe it."

The finality in her tone made him narrow his eyes. "Then you tell me, Marcie: What *was* she doing out there?"

Marcie shook her head, but slowly, almost as if in a trance. "I'm not sure. But if you let me talk to her, I can find out."

He pursed his lips again. "I haven't even questioned her myself, not even informally."

"So?"

"So, I've got people to answer to. You don't. I will, however, offer this: Come with me. Be there when I do it. That way, at least you'll see we're on the up and up."

"Under what circumstances?

"Behind the glass. Unofficially." He looked at her again. "What do you say?"

She nodded, but said nothing.

Marcie gazed listlessly into the one-way mirror and watched Tull in the interrogation room. Bare white walls. One desk in white laminate, one chair upon which he sat. On the desk was a folder and a pen. Beside them were two glasses of iced water.

The door opened and Annie appeared, the strong-jawed and deeply tanned face of a guard behind her. Although obviously exhausted, Annie seemed remarkably unafraid.

"Over there," Tull said, pointing at a spot in front of the desk, establishing control.

Annie moved obediently forward and stood there, watching.

Tull opened the folder and pretended to read it.

All the while Marcie thought the man was slime, just like his father. Better educated, more presentable, but still the same fetid waste.

Tull finally looked up. He tried to meet Annie's eyes, but they were too much for him and he cleared his throat. "So, Annie, what were you doing wandering around the camp at night? Taking a little stroll when you should have been in bed?"

"I wanted to escape," she said, her voice flat.

Marcie immediately noticed the difference. It wasn't Annie's normal voice. There was some edge to it—a fatalism, perhaps.

"And how were you planning to do that? Fly over the perimeter fence?" he said, attempting a smile.

"I don't know," she replied. "I wanted to see if there was a way. I wanted to look and find a way."

"You must have had some ideas."

"I thought maybe of stowing away on one of the freight trucks that carry paper to the city."

She's lying, Marcie thought. I know her as well as I know myself, and she's lying through her teeth.

"But you weren't anywhere near the truck bays," he said.

"I wanted to look at the perimeter first, to see if there was a way through there."

"How? I find that hard to believe, Annie. You've seen the perimeter a thousand times. You know there's no way through it. Why did you suddenly think there might be?"

Annie shrugged her slim shoulders. "I don't know. I thought there might be a way."

"But you weren't prepared for an escape, Annie. You were wearing these clothes. You had no food, no water. Nothing."

"I guess I wasn't thinking very clearly."

"Was anyone with you?" Tull asked. "Anyone help you plan this?"

"No, I was alone," Annie said.

Another lie, Marcie thought. And this time the realization sent a definite chill through her body.

Someone had been with her! Who and why? What had been going on? Did it have something to do with what Annie had been saying to her that something was about to happen? What the hell *had* happened out there last night?

Tull tried another tack. He pushed one of the glasses of water across the table toward her. "Have a drink, Annie. I know you haven't had anything since last night. Must be thirsty."

She picked up the glass and finished its contents in one swallow.

"You know, Annie, I don't think you understand what's happening here. Escape is a very serious offense, usually punishable by execution. Did you know that?"

"Yes," she said.

"Well, if you were doing something else out there, maybe you should tell me. It might go easier for you."

"It's like I said."

Tull looked at her and scowled. "Annie, there are other ways to question you. If you're hiding anything, you'd better tell me now."

"I've told you everything," she said.

"I hope so. I really hope so." He closed the folder and pointed at the door. "Go. You'll be taken back to your cell. I'll be talking to you again. Very soon."

Annie began to turn, then stopped and looked directly at the mirror on the wall. To Marcie, the moment seemed to last forever, but then Annie completed her turn, went to the door, and opened it.

What the hell was going on? Marcie thought, almost panicked.

Tull got up a moment later and left the door, the folder in his hands. He came into the room.

"Well?" he asked.

"I don't know," Marcie said, as calmly as she could.

"You know her. Was she telling the truth?"

"Yes," Marcie said.

Tull looked at her appraisingly, then he nodded. "I don't believe you, and I don't believe her. And I'm going to find out what's going on here."

• • •

Marcie worked in the shipping office attached to the printing plant. Most of her day was spent filling out invoices on the computer. It was, luckily, a job that took no thought, for this afternoon her mind was seething.

Annie had definitely been lying and probably, she guessed, protecting someone. But who and from what? What the hell had the kid been doing out there at three in the morning?

The first person to tell her of Annie's plight had been a kid who worked in the print shop. David. Obviously love-struck and very worried, he told her that Annie had been caught trying to escape. "You're a friend of hers, right? Can you do anything to help her? I hear you got some pull. Can you help her?" That's when she'd gone to see Tull.

Did the boy know anything else? She thought back to their conversation and concluded that he hadn't. Besides, he looked incapable of guile. Just a nice young kid who adored Annie.

Who, then?

She sensed the presence behind her and turned from the computer.

He was an inmate she hadn't noticed before: medium height, lean, with dark hair, late twenties or early thirties. Nondescript, except for his presence, which showed some kind of rare willingness to face whatever he had to face, the power. And then, of course, there were his eyes, totally unreadable, deep and dark.

"Yes?" she said.

"You're Marcie."

"Yes. Who are you?"

"Is Annie all right?"

She opened her mouth, then closed it. He knew. He knew what this was all about. He was the one.

"Who are you?"

"A friend. If you're a friend of Annie's like I heard, then I'm your friend. Is she all right?"

"For now."

"What did she tell them?"

"A stupid story. That she was trying to escape."

"And they don't believe her," he said, half to himself. "Have they started the tough questioning yet?"

"They probably will. Late tonight," she said bitterly. "Tull likes to put them under the machine late at night, him and that shrink lady."

"What do you mean by 'late'?" he asked.

"When they're tired. They don't let them sleep. Then Tull goes and takes a nap and starts in around midnight or so."

"All right. Thank you," he said, and he turned to leave.

"Wait!" she said and stared into those eyes. "What are you going to do?"

She was shocked at her own question. He was an inmate, just like her. Powerless. What on earth did she think he could do? And yet it made sense, because if anyone could do anything it would be him.

He took a step back and turned those eyes on her again. For a moment he just looked. But although she couldn't read those eyes, she knew that they were seeing her, evaluating, deciding.

"She's going to be all right," he said finally.

"What can I do?" she asked, believing him.

"You have a room of your own, right?"

She nodded.

"What hut?"

She described the location of her room.

"When I need you I'll come to you." He moved off.

God, she thought, understanding finally what Annie had been talking about. It has finally happened. Something has finally happened.

CHAPTER 28

The message reached Gray at nine that evening. They were in a deep gully three miles from Mojave, hunkered down, nursing their weapons. Some quietly talked about nothing, while others gazed out across the flatland that seemed to dissolve into the blackness a thousand yards beyond the dunes. Although it was cold, with winds from the northeast, no one complained about it, or even mentioned it.

"He wants us to move it up to midnight, four hours ahead of schedule," Bill Casey said.

"You're sure?"

"He sent it twice. Very fast, of course, but twice."

Casey had developed the transmitter they had given to Klein. A simple affair, it had only about fifteen settings, each one corresponding to a possible scenario, a quick series of spurts. "Cancel the mission." "Move it a day ahead." "Move it a day later." "Move it an hour earlier." And so on. Simple, and so fast it was virtually untraceable.

They had been planning to hit the camp at four in the morning, that hour when sleep was deepest, dreams the heaviest, and detection least likely. Midnight, on the other hand, was fraught with peril. People grew nervous at midnight. And with that came a paranoid alertness. But Klein would have his reasons, and they would be compelling. Besides, as understood, he was the man on the spot, and it was entirely his call.

Gray glanced up at the sky, at the sliver of a moon through the clouds. "What kind of an approach does midnight give us?" he asked.

Casey shook his head. "You mean time-wise? It's tight, but not impossible."

"And the outward patrols?"

"Outward patrols are not a problem."

He turned to Maggie Sharp and Arbunckle on his left. "You heard?" was all he said.

Arbunckle replied with a curt nod. "Midnight means we move in about fifty minutes."

Gray returned his gaze to the sky again—to the clouds churning in from the north, to the moon fighting for a moment of life, to what might have been a hawk circling on the jet stream.

"Then let's do it."

They moved out in stages, first almost shuffling, gradually forming into a ragged line—weapons locked, clips taped, infrareds on wide scan. Now and again, things slithered from their path: snakes, lizards, things. There were also whispers of the wind through the scrub and the hollow beating of rising wings. But, for the most part, there were no sounds at all beyond their footsteps and the steady click-click of the scanners. Although the tension was still palpable, Gray was not worried. In fact, he was pleased, because he wanted the edge, wanted the nerves tight, hard. His core people had been tested time and time again; he had no doubts about them. Some of the others had proven themselves during the armory raid; the remainder would prove themselves later that night.

In order to minimize their discernible size, they broke into three groups at four thousand yards—the first led by Arbunckle, the other two by Sharp and Gray. At a thousand yards, the distance between each team was widened to a hundred and fifty yards, then out two hundred, then back one-fifty. Although the heat-seekers, registered to 98.6°, picked up two figures at the thousand-yard mark, the readings proved to be nothing.

According to Klein, the Mojave facility maintained only one TRU-ship, one of the older X-20s. Now and again, generally after attempted breaks, the ship was launched on three-mile patrols. There were also a couple of desert-adapted Marauders, Klein had said, sometimes launched on scouting expeditions along the tracks leading from the camp into the desert, although rarely at night.

For John Gray, walking along the rocky surfaces and descending into the sandy washes reminded him of another journey years earlier. Then he had been running for his life in the opposite direction, toward the mountains, a .357 Ruger magnum in one hand, a canteen filled with half a liter of water in his other, a survival knife in his belt, and four sticks of gum in his pocket. Afraid, yes, but filled with a savage will, the seeds of the same will that drove him tonight, back the way he had once come.

This time, however, it was different. This time he had people and weapons and surprise on his side.

They reached a ravine four hundred yards from Mojave's perimeter at eleven o'clock, first Gray's group, followed quickly by Arbunckle and Maggie Sharp. From here, there were two distinct visions of the compound: the twin towers along the western perimeter and the chain link against the sky. Then very faintly, like a shifting cable of moonlight: the lights.

"Figure we have seven minutes once Klein cuts the power," Gray said softly. "If you got a problem with the fence, then cut the razor wire and go over it. After seven minutes, the emergency generator kicks in, and so do the floodlights."

"How do you want to take the tower guards?" Maggie asked.

Gray looked at her. "As quietly as possible."

"And the backup?" Arbunckle asked.

"Should be minimal. Most of them will be in for the night or hanging out in the admin compound. Although once we've dealt with them, Maggie's got to get up on that rooftop with shoulder launchers. The main thing is to make sure nothing leaves the camp. Their communications will be down, so they'll try and make a run for help, probably after twenty or thirty minutes, when they realize how bad it is."

"And what happens if they start hitting back at the prisoner barracks?" Casey said from behind Gray's left shoulder.

Gray nodded. "If we can stop it, we stop it. Otherwise people are going to get hurt."

Gray turned back to Arbunckle. "Either way, though, once we're in, you can start moving your people around to the southern huts so that we're flanking them. When they come running out of the guards' quarters, they're going to be easy targets. Make the most of it. While you're doing that, I'll be sending a missile or two right through the front door of the admin building."

As a final question, Arbunckle said, "You tink de people in dere are in any kind of shape to help us?"

Gray's lips grew tight and he stared into some private vision before answering. "Believe me," he said finally, "they'll rise to the occasion. Even if they don't know it, they've all been waiting a long time for this moment."

CHAPTER 29

The art of stealth, as Danny Klein had once learned it in Japan, had to do with becoming one with the available environment, merging into it so thoroughly you were virtually indistinguishable from it. As white was the absence of color, and black the preponderance of it, he had learned to use both dark and light in which to become invisible. It was simply a matter of harmonizing with what was available.

When he dropped from his window half an hour before midnight, the moon was obscured by clouds and all surfaces in the camp were shades of gray, mottled by the sweeping searchlights and shafts of dim illumination that fell from windows in the administration building and guards' quarters. Lights had long since been extinguished in the inmate huts.

Klein didn't hesitate when he hit the ground. Almost in the same motion he moved directly along a line of shadows toward the tool hut where he had left his supplies. When he reached it, he opened the lock with one smooth flick of the wrist, entered the hut, and closed the door behind him.

Quickly he went through his bag of tricks. He checked the machine pistol and the grenades, leaving them in the bag. He put the watch around his wrist, then strapped the knife to his back so that an easy reach over his right shoulder would grasp it. He wouldn't need the other weapons quite yet.

Bag in one hand, he returned to the night.

The communications building sat directly behind the main administration offices, connected by about thirty feet of concrete pathway. The giant antenna protruding from the roof allowed long-distance radio contact, but there was also, of course, a telephone linkage system. Here too was the electrical system, which dispersed power to the rest of the camp.

The emergency generator was located in the administration building itself, but it had a limited capacity. As far as Klein had been able to discover, it would power the admin building and some of the searchlights, leaving the rest of the camp in the dark.

There were always two men on duty in the communications building, sometimes three. The eight-hour shift changed at 10:00 P.M. It would have been better to approach them at three or four, when they would be fighting the temptation of sleep, but he had little choice other than to do it now.

He circled around the building, approaching from the back, sidling up to the double doors used for bringing equipment through. They were, as he had found during a previous reconnoitering, unlocked.

He slipped inside and stood in the gloomy hallway. It led straight down the center of the building, from back to front door. To his right was the power room. He could hear the steady hum of machinery from where he stood. There could be one man in inside, although it wasn't always a guarded area. To his left, farther down the hall, was the communications room, housing the radio and telephone equipment. There would definitely be two men on duty there—one operating the radio and one on the main telephone switchboard.

He reached behind his back and withdrew the double-edged Shafer-Tor survival blade—black finish, with a taped hasp, perfectly balanced.

After placing the bag on the floor against the wall, he began to move without hesitation toward the communications room, his movements swift and fluid, the knife in his right hand, his left free and open. He moved like mercury, his back straight, his right foot crossing over his left.

For a second he hesitated at the doorway, just long enough to hear the sounds of two men talking, one of them derisively, the other quietly resentful.

"You couldn't win yourself a funeral with a hand like that," said one.

"It ain't over till it's over," said the other.

Klein came through the doorway like a wind, blowing them back with the force of his entrance. They sat at a table, two of them, cards in their hands, confusion in their eyes.

The one on the right was a large man—black-haired, thick-featured, with a bull neck; the other was small, in his late forties, as thin as a rail.

He didn't give them time to think. In that same liquid motion he was suddenly on them, the knife in his right hand slashing across the throat of the larger man—one motion that opened it up in a haze of pumping red.

But almost in the same movement his other hand arced toward the smaller man, the edge of his palm slicing just below his nose, sending the bones into his brain.

Both men hit the floor at the same moment. For them, it was over.

Klein swung around, went back out the door, and moved fast down the hall to the power room, the blood-stained knife still in his right hand.

He opened the door and stepped inside, a swiveling glance taking in the banks of circuitry. Other than that, the room was empty. Returning to the hallway, he picked up his bag and took it back into the room.

With a knowledgeable glance around at the equipment, he chose his targets, two areas where all the circuits integrated. He took two of the grenades from the bag and glanced at his watch. Setting the timers, he placed them.

Back in the communications room, ignoring the bodies on the floor, he did the same with two more grenades, one for the radio and the other for the telephone equipment.

This done, he went to the bodies. He turned over the man whose throat he had cut, paying no attention to the gaping bloody mess, and lifted an Armscore machine pistol from the holster at his waist. He did the same to the other man and finally also scooped up a Gillette M-90 that leaned against the radio desk.

Then he left the building, moving out the back door and through the shadows.

Annie Fumito's cell was little more than a black box. A hard wooden bench ran along one wall, but it was only two feet long, not enough to lie on. There had once been a light bulb, but it had long since burned out, and now the only illumination was the dim glow of a light somewhere down the hall. There were no toilet facilities in the cell, and when she had asked a guard if she could go to the bathroom, the reply was a cruel laugh. She had urinated finally by squatting on the floor, the liquid running under her feet.

She had no idea how long she had been there; time seemed to be beside the point anyway, just so much useless speculation. Nor did she think very deeply about what was going to happen to her. It was likely that she would either be tortured or killed or both. There didn't seem to be much room for speculation in that scenario either. As far as she knew, for it would have been brought up by now, they had not found Klein out at the perimeter after they had caught her. And, in essence, she also knew that to be the only truly important fact, for the survival of many depended upon him, while her survival or lack of it would affect nobody else. At least not for very long.

When the guard appeared, Annie was trying to sleep, sitting upright, head back against the rough stucco wall, eyes closed. First there was the sound of the electric bolt, then the approaching steps.

"All right, outta here."

It was a guard named Avis, a fat black woman with short hair and a thick neck. She carried a stun prod in her right hand.

Annie rose wearily and moved toward the door. Avis stepped back and gestured down the hall. "Gonna visit the warden in the shock room, baby. He wants to have a talk with you."

Annie felt nothing, just trudged on ahead, through another series of locked doors and down another hallway.

"Left," the guard said.

When they entered the room, the lights almost blinded her for a brief moment; then she saw the machine, a long bed with straps hanging from the sides. Beside it stood the camp shrink, Dr. Palmer, looking radiant as always.

"Thank you, Avis," Palmer said, and then she smiled at Annie and patted the surface beside her. "You can lie down here and have a little rest now, dear."

Annie glanced around and for the first time noticed Tull. He sat on a chair inside a glass booth, his sly eyes fixed on her, a small smile on his mouth. He looked like a king on his throne.

"Ah, yes, the warden wants to ask you a few questions." She patted the machine again. "Lie down here. They'll be much easier for you to answer."

Annie looked at the machine, observing the dials, the helmet that would fit over her head. She knew what it did, had heard the stories from other inmates, had even seen the victims, senseless creatures who wandered rotely through what remained of their lives. But still she felt nothing—no fear, no apprehension. Nothing. It was as if she existed in an untouchable void.

She moved closer to the machine, allowed the shrink to take her shoulders and gently push her back. Below her she felt the surface move, adjust to the shape of her body. She closed her eyes then and wished she could sleep. She was hardly aware of the straps moving around her legs and wrists, and she certainly didn't care.

"Isn't that nice and relaxing," a lilting voice said in her ear. And in spite of its concerned and calming tone, Annie was able to sense the evil in that voice, and she suddenly opened her eyes and saw what was about to happen and felt fear for the first time.

"Yes," the voice cooed, and she saw the ugliness behind that pretty face above her. "We're going to be just fine."

Then came the first explosion. And the face above her disappeared in a sudden blackness as the lights went out.

CHAPTER 30

Having pulled the dead shift, Howard Rollins arrived at the tower at four minutes before midnight. Two minutes later Andy Speckler joined him, lugging under his arm a Spectralite Hot 'n' Cold converter filled with foul coffee. In his other hand he juggled a Hot Marauder video card.

It was cold, the wind kicking up sand beyond the perimeter and whistling through the chain-link fence.

Upon entering the tower, Speckler turned on the television set and rapidly flipped through the channels: *The Joey Barker Show* had Dr. Ingmar Dresser discussing her book on the sexual proclivities of the Oriental woman; a rerun of *Cats Buckler: Urban Enforcer*; and *Lotto Free for All!*

"You know what I miss?" Speckler said, tilting back in the polyurethane deck chair, boots on the plastic console. "Those old cartoons they used to show. You know, where the guy gets it over the head with a frying pan, and his head kinda turns into a frying pan, and he's got those birds flying around him. Or what about when the guy gets run over by a steamroller, and he's like flattened to like a quarter of an inch, or maybe an eighth of an inch. And then the duck comes in and peels him off, and he's—"

"Look," Rollins interrupted, "just shut up, okay?"

"All right, what about this?" Speckler said, changing to a rerun of *PsychDick!*, the adventures of psychiatrist-detective Dr. Mildred Birch.

"Whatever," Rollins said.

"Oh, this is the one where she busts this Devo, except he's

183

not really a Devo but an undercover Corporate enforcer. Only she doesn't know that, and then they—what the fuck?"

As the screen went blank with a muffled thump a hundred yards away.

Rollins scrambled to his feet. "What the fuck was that?" he asked, peering out through the plexiglass. "All the lights are gone."

Another deadened explosion reverberated across the yard.

Very calm and cool, he turned to his partner. "Andy boy, I think we got a condition three."

But Speckler was already reaching for the telephone, while his eyes grew marginally wider.

"Dead," he whispered into the receiver.

Through the wind came sounds of something possibly scraping against the wire, then what might have been the click-click of steel against steel.

"You see anything?" Speckler hissed.

"I don't know. I don't think so. Hand me the infrareds."

Without turning from the plexiglass, Rollins extended a hand behind him, took hold of the Polaroid-Fuji infrared goggles, and put them up to his eyes.

After a moment of dead silence: "Holy shit!"

"What?" Speckler said.

"You're not going to believe this."

"What!?"

"We got at least—"

Broken by the sound of shattering plexiglass and an intense burst of wind.

"Oh, Jesus, oh, fucking Jesus."

Rollins slowly turned, his hands pressed against the fist-sized hole in his chest.

And then at last, as the faint human whistling broke above the wind, Speckler crawled under the laminated console and tightly squeezed shut his eyes.

Seventy yards along the perimeter from where Speckler now lay shivering, the last Whistler slipped through the thirty-six-inch gash in the chain-link fence. Twenty-five yards ahead, among the first rank of supply sheds, another fifteen Whistlers were melting into the shadows.

Beyond the sheds lay the low gates to the prisoners' compound and then the outlines of the barracks, where at least a dozen eyes peered through the screened windows. While closer to the administration building, an obviously terrified woman kept shouting: "Hey, Jodie, is that you? What's going on out there? Is that you?"

Also wakened from a restless sleep by the echo of those blasts, Marcie caught only glimpses of shadows from her window. Once or twice among the sheds she saw what seemed to be an undulating dark mass scurrying against the flagstones. Then briefly, so fast she could not be sure, she caught a glimpse of a sweat-drenched face.

When she heard Klein's voice behind her, however, she calmly turned and said only, "This is really happening, isn't it?"

Without replying, Klein stepped into the room, sank to his haunches, and gently laid a duffel bag down, unzipping it to reveal a black mass of neatly packed weapons.

"Who do you know that can use these?" he asked.

She looked down at the Gillette M-90s. "How many of you are there?"

"Enough. Now tell me, who can use them?"

She pressed a hand to her head and said, "Jesus! I don't know. Morez, the little Mex, maybe Kolinsky, and that other guy that used to be a cop. What's his name? Pelican. I don't know how many others."

"Are most of them still in Two?"

"Probably. I don't know."

"If I take you there, will you talk to them?"

Marcie rose slowly to her feet, started to the door, then hesitated and said, "This really is happening."

"Does anyone know what the fuck is going on?" asked Carl Heldt as he jammed a fresh magazine into his M-90.

In reply, Frankie Daly only smirked. "They cause trouble, we kick ass. What else you want to know?"

In all, nine guards had gathered in the marshaling yard under Phil Post's command: Heldt, Daily, the Cliver twins, Donny Shore, and two kids just in from District Command. Although there were definitely voices from the adjacent barracks and possibly figures lining up along the eastern perimeter, Post was suddenly very conscious that he and his nine would be the first to respond to whatever the disturbance was.

"Listen up," Post said. "I don't know what the hell is going on out there, but any inmates moving around are dead inmates. We're gonna go in through the main gates. We're going to stay together, and we're not going to be stupid. You see movement on the grounds, you drop 'em. You do not break rank and you keep your mouths shut. Any questions?"

"What if we're not just talking about inmates?" Heldt asked.

But Post just looked at him and said, "Let's move out."

There were sixty yards of relatively open ground beyond the guards' compound, and the squad moved out at an easy pace. In addition to the standard-mounted night-vision systems on the M-90s, Post also carried a pair of those Polaroid-Fuji infrared goggles loosely around his neck. Every few yards he lifted them to his eyes and scanned the approach to the inmates' compound.

Although Post had seen action in a couple of arenas, including the Chicago riots of 2012, he was not what one would call a seasoned soldier. Thus when he first glimpsed the figure peering from the corrugated rooftop of a tool shed just before the prisoners' compound, he initially wondered why a maintenance man would be working past midnight.

His next thought concerned the riveter resting on the shoulder of the man—which he almost simultaneously realized was not a man but a woman, and that the riveter was a Remco minigun in harness.

In the same split second, as he began to lift his M-90, it also occurred to him that if in fact he was facing a Remco, there was nothing—no order, no response—that would make a bit of difference right now.

Because at eight hundred rounds a minute he didn't even have time for his next thought.

It was an extended burst, sounding almost like a buzz saw, literally severing at least three of them in half—the others pulverized beyond recognition.

At the same time Phil Post stopped thinking about the incongruity of maintenance men, Harve Gratis began to think about diving for the floor—pressing his face hard into the linoleum and shutting his eyes real tight.

Because having just stepped out of the Number Nine guard barracks and raised his eyes to the eastern perimeter to see a line of five advancing silhouettes, he next saw the white burst of an incoming Krause-Nova shoulder-launched missile.

In all there were thirty-four members of the Mojave Correctional Facility guard unit still in the Number Nine barracks, grabbing weapons and boots amidst shouts and whispers, when the Krause-Nova snaked through the doorway.

Although Harve Gratis, now flat on the floor, could not actually see the explosion, he felt it—first the hot blast of air, then the lung-wrenching concussion, and finally the rain of what he prayed was not human debris.

There were also screams from the west end of the barracks yard, where bursts of M-90 fire sprayed into reeling shadows of guards. Then quite clearly, lifting his eyes at last, Gratis saw the withering effects of at least nine flechettes ripping through the head and shoulders of a guard they called the Growler. For a moment, possibly a second or two, the Growler seemed merely stunned, then almost amused. But when he finally sank to the flagstones, his face was no less than a bloody pulp.

Eventually, after what must have been another sixty or seventy seconds, it occurred to Gratis that he really should get going . . . maybe slither on into the drainage ditch or one of the tool sheds. But the moment he attempted to shift his right leg, the dull horror of it all came home: he had no legs.

As a last thought before sinking into unconsciousness, he supposed that he may have also lost his left arm, because how else could he account for all the pumping blood?

Despite the reverberation of blasts from the guards' compound it was still relatively quiet while Klein and Marcie faced some sixty anxious inmates. Some were frightened, others merely confused. Still others, the fifteen or twenty listening to Klein's soft and measured words, were simply eager.

"All right, what you're looking at is a Gillette M-90. This is your safety on, this off. You have fifty flechettes to the clip, two clips taped to the butt. Don't worry about aiming, just point it."

When he extended the first weapon to an outstretched hand, a voice from the ring of faces whispered, "I want one too."

Kolinsky held his weapon in his hand and briefly shut his eyes, while Pelican and the wiry Morez merely smiled.

The boy David held out his hand, and Klein hesitated only for a second before giving him a weapon.

There was another series of rolling explosions from two

hundred yards across the compound, then softer voices from just beyond the barracks door.

There were flames visible from the window, and when Marcie felt Klein's hand on her shoulder, she asked, "Who are you people?"

"We got to move."

She turned to face him. "Look, I want to know who you are."

It was a question that echoed in dozens of faces around them, some still sitting on their cots, some clutching the weapons, and an ancient figure muttering to himself in the corner.

"Who are you?"

"You know who I am, Marcie," came a soft voice from the doorway.

She half turned, stepping forward, straining to see through the darkness. Another step closer. Then finally, barely above a whisper, saying, "Johnny?"

"Hello, Marcie," said Gray.

A lot of things passed through Marcie's mind as she moved out with Gray and Klein and some fifty inmates through the compound toward the guard barracks. She thought about a little Johnny so many years ago, huddled on a cot, asking about his parents. She thought about rumors she had heard from nearly a decade before that they had never found him in the desert, and of later rumors of the seeds of rebellion in the city. She thought about the fact that it had been a long, long time since a man had ever held her and since she had tasted real milk.

In the end, however, all she said to Klein was: "What about Annie?"

CHAPTER 31

From deep within some secret storehouse of memories, Tull vaguely recalled having once dreamed of this moment: explosions in the darkness beyond the window, curtains billowing with blasts of hot air, a young girl strapped to an operating table, but without so much as a spark of power to charge her up. There had also been something about a severed hand on the flagstones, and very briefly, in the flash of a flame gun, he had indeed seen what looked like a human hand.

"Don't you think we'd better do something?" asked Palmer from the shadows behind him. "Did you hear me, Hank? I said, I think we'd better do something!"

Tull turned from the window to face the woman. Although her voice had been remarkably restrained, her eyes were obviously filled with terror, and he saw that those long, slim fingers were twisted into painful knots. All he said, however, was: "What the hell do you expect me to do, Lilith?"

There were echoes of more flechettes whistling in from surrounding rooftops, glancing off corrugated steel and brickwork. There were also more screams, and somebody quite close kept shouting: *I don't believe this! I don't fucking believe this!*

Tull moved through the doorway and into the operating room, where the Fumito girl lay unmoving in the gloom. When the explosions had first ripped through the night, she had briefly whispered a name. Once the shooting had started, however, she had grown very still and very quiet.

Tull stepped to the side of the table, gently brushed the hair from her forehead, and idly tugged on the straps that restrained her. In response, she looked at him, but she might have been looking right through him.

"You know exactly what's going on, don't you?" Tull smiled. "You knew from the start, didn't you? Those people out there, those weapons—you knew from the word go."

The girl shifted her gaze slightly to the left but otherwise offered no reply.

"Not that it matters, really," Tull continued. "Still, who would have ever thought? Who would have—"

Another explosion, no more than sixty or seventy feet beyond the walls, sent shards of glass flying through the outer office and Palmer fell to her knees, screaming: "For godsakes, Hank, we have got to do something!"

Tull, however, merely smiled. "Yes, I suppose you're right again, Lilith. We have got to do something." Then, returning his gaze to the girl, but still faintly smiling: "How about it, honey? Shall we do something?" Then, slowly extending his right hand to her throat, the fingers very gradually increasing the pressure: "Shall we do something?"

"All right, you tell me," Gray breathed. "Just tell me what you want to do."

Klein ran a hand across his mouth and peered out across the assembly yard to the dull glow of burning barracks. "I want to try and get Annie out of there," he finally replied.

Gray also rose and peered out above the remnants of a blown tool shed, the twisted remains of an ATV, and the less identifiable debris still smoldering in heaps across the flagstones. Still closer to the administration compound lay what may have been the charred outlines of guards: limbs twisted into impossible angles, mouths stretched in silent screams.

"How much time are we talking about?" Gray finally replied.

Klein shrugged. "Say fifteen, twenty minutes to get in, another ten to get out."

"With what kind of backup?"

"It doesn't matter. Just give me time."

"But even if she's still alive, and do you know—"

"I know," Klein said.

There were sounds of footsteps approaching from between the ranks of storage sheds, then the double click of a magazine locking into place. A moment later, three faces appeared out of the gloom: Casey, Vermeer, Jackie Arbunckle. Behind them stood at least twenty crouched figures of inmates armed with a variety of weapons.

"According to the Mags we got dem real centered now, mon," Arbunckle said. "In fact, according to Mags, we got 'em right where we want 'em."

Gray glanced up to the surrounding rooft·s but saw only what appeared to be more dead. "Where is she?"

Arbunckle cocked his head slightly to the left. "Up on de tower dere. She up on de tower with dat shoulder launch, and she say dat one of dem sixty-sixty's hit da concrete and must have blown about fifty of 'em back to never-never land. And now de rest is just waiting for it. Dey just be sitting dere waiting for it. Anyway, dat's what Maggie say."

"So how many does she think are left?"

Arbunckle closed one eye in an exaggerated wink. "Oh, maybe fifty or sixty. But dey be centered, mon. Dey be pinned down and centered real fine."

"And Tull?"

Arbunckle shook his head. "No, mon. No sign of him, mon."

Gray exchanged another glance with Klein, then turned to the faces behind him. Finally meeting the still gaze of Paolo Cruz, he crossed twenty feet of rubble-strewn sand and knelt down to the boy's side.

"How about it, Paolo?"

The boy lowered his gaze to a near perfect circle he had drawn in the sand, motionless, staring, fingering a pebble he must have picked up without thinking. Then, finally drawing in a deep breath and exhaling through his teeth: "I think Mr. Klein is right. I think that girl is still alive."

"Can you tell me where?"

Another long moment's silence, with no other movement than the action of his thumb and forefinger across the pebble. "A room. She's in a room with the fat man and a blond woman. They've got her on a table, and they're thinking about hurting her. She's still alive and still strong."

"And what about the room, Paolo? Tell me about the room."

"It's white, but it's dark. Broken glass on the floor, and curtains moving back and forth."

"And do you know exactly how—"

"Over there." He lifted an arm, extended a finger. "Over there, beyond those barracks. That's where she is."

Gray rose to his feet again and moved back to where Klein still knelt among the shattered concrete. "Okay," he said. "Twenty minutes in, ten minutes to bring her back. But meanwhile I'm going to move these people in from the north, so watch it when you're coming out."

Klein lifted his M-90 and dropped the safety. "Thanks. I appreciate it."

"Oh, and Danny?"

Klein stopped, motionless, waiting.

"If it's at all possible, how about saving Tull for me?"

Tull released the girl's throat and slowly turned to face Avery Wallace in the doorway. In addition to lacerations along the man's left forearm, the deputy had apparently injured his hand. There was also a lot of blood on his trousers, although probably not his own.

"I think we'd better talk about negotiating some kind of surrender," Wallace said.

Tull pressed a finger to his lower lip, then moved to the vinyl sofa and sat down. "Come again, Avery?"

"Surrender, Warden. I think it's time to discuss a surrender."

"With whom? With a foolish little brigade of inmates that have somehow managed to—"

"Look, I don't think you understand. We have suffered over sixty percent casualties, and now they've got us entirely surrounded out there. They can drop whatever they want on us at will, including those goddamn shoulder-launched things. Now, you want to play Custer's Last Stand, that's up to you. But right now we've probably got about ten minutes before they start coming at us in force, and we want to talk surrender. Do you understand the situation now?"

Tull rose to his feet again, his eyes once more fixed on the Fumito girl. "You know, Avery, I never liked you. I never liked you one bit."

But Wallace simply shut his eyes, letting the air hiss out between clenched teeth. "Jesus, you still don't get it, do you? There is no . . . way . . . out. They've got the roads sealed. They've got the perimeters sealed. They've blown the chopper and most of the ATVs. Now, we either call it a night or we die. Do you understand?"

Tull also briefly shut his eyes, idly running a finger along the girl's forehead. "Of course I understand. We are standing at the focal point of history. Right now. You, me, this little girl, Dr. Palmer, those men out there—all at the focal point of a historical change in the tide of this century." Then, suddenly turning to face the man again: "Give me your weapon, Avery. Come on, hand it over. I'm going to show you how one rides a tidal wave of history."

For at least five minutes after Tull had stalked out of the room, Lilith Palmer remained fixed in the corner: back flat against the plaster, eyes shut tight. Then, following another long peal of autofire from across the courtyard, she sank to the linoleum and began to crawl on her hands and knees. When she passed through the door of the operating room, another burst of screaming flechettes sent her flat to the floor. But eventually, by degrees, she rose to her feet and approached the table.

"Oh, I know what you're thinking," she breathed softly to the girl. "You're thinking that at this point it doesn't matter whether you live or die, just so long as they get me. But that's not going to happen, sweetheart. Uh-uh. You and I are going to get ourselves the hell out of here right now."

She eased the restraining straps from Annie's wrists, then slowly lifted the girl's shoulders until she was sitting up. When Annie responded with an aching moan, Palmer whispered, "Sure, hurts a little." Then, yanking Annie's wrists behind her back, Palmer cinched the straps taut again. "Now you just sit tight for a moment."

Palmer found two Remington-Steiger conversions in the cabinet in Tull's office: a nine-flechette load on top and a scatter charge below. She also found a roll of masking tape in a drawer but finally decided on a coat hanger.

When she returned to the girl, she worked quickly, methodically, occasionally whispering to herself. She wrapped the coat hanger around Annie's neck, twisted the end tight, then looped the other end around the finger guard of the Remington-Steiger. Then testing the play, while still softly whispering, she unstrapped the girl's ankles and helped her from the table.

Passing a shattered mirror in the outer office, she caught a quick glimpse of herself: eyes slightly red around the edges, long strands of hair hanging from her bun, the muzzle of that Remington held firmly to the girl's slender throat by means of the coat hanger . . . and all the while thinking: *Well, Sweet Mother of Jesus, will you look at me.*

It was cold in the courtyard, and the winds brought a stench of burning flesh. Someone not far away kept murmuring: "Oh, stinking hell. Oh, stinking hell." But given the wire around her throat and the pressure of the muzzle, Annie could not turn her head.

She wasn't frightened; not really. Her head had been throbbing for hours and her mouth felt as dry as sand. She also desperately wished that the doctor would stop yanking the shotgun, because the wire hurt like hell. But as far as living or dying was concerned, she was no longer certain that she even cared. She had done her duty.

They paused in the shadows of another blown barracks, and she heard the doctor whisper: "Now, listen real carefully, sugar plum. We're going to keep walking until we get to the motor pool. Then we're going to find some way of getting the hell on out of here. And if anyone tries to stop us . . ." She gently yanked on that coat hanger: "Well, I think you get the picture. Let's hope they do too."

There were more voices past the barracks, a guard shouting: "We are coming out! I repeat, we are coming out!" But the only response was more autofire.

Then quite calmly, from the deeper darkness, someone said, "Stop right there!"

Annie felt another gentle tug on her throat, then heard the doctor hissing in her ear again: "Okay, sugar pie, don't screw up now." Then, louder to the unseen figures in the gloom, her voice more high pitched than she wanted it to sound: "You want to see this little baby's brains? Is that what you people want?"

Three figures emerged from the blackness ahead: two inmates that Annie had never known well, and a wiry Mexican named Morez. Although they had leveled their weapons straight at Palmer's belly, none of them seemed ready to fire.

"Go ahead, gentlemen," Palmer said calmly. "Do it. Come on. Do it. Only I can't be responsible for any muscular reactions."

Morez may have whispered something to the others, and there was the sound of a dropping safety. But when Palmer finally started forward, shoving Annie with her, the inmates merely stepped aside.

"See, little honey pie," Palmer whispered. "See how easy it is when you're loved."

But even as the woman continued whispering, mumbling something about muscular reactions and response to impact, a second voice was sounding in Annie's ear: flat, dry, almost like something from a dream.

"Let her go," said Klein.

Palmer stopped, and Annie felt that wire digging into her throat again. Then she heard Palmer's voice hot on her neck. "I know you. You're the new one."

"That's right," Klein said. "I'm the new one."

He took another step closer, then another and another, until he was barely three feet away: eyes locked on the doctor's eyes, hands at his sides.

"Back . . . off," Palmer hissed. "You got it? Back . . . off, or I blow this little girl's head right off her shoulders."

But Klein merely shrugged. "Fine. Do it."

Annie felt another tug on that wire, jerking her head slightly to the left, so that now she too could see Klein . . . could look directly into his eyes, into the nothingness.

"I'm serious, mister," Palmer sneered. "Back off or I'll blow her head off."

But by this time Klein had already raised his right arm, leveling the muzzle of that M-90 directly into Palmer's eyes. "Go on, Doctor. Pull the trigger."

While Palmer shouted, "Look, I am serious. Back off. Back off right now or I'll blow—"

Then although no shot was fired, the scream that tore out of her couldn't have been more agonized . . . as Klein's left arm whipped up in a dark blur, and the eight-inch blade extending from his sleeve severed Palmer's right hand at the wrist.

Annie caught a quick glimpse of the woman's reeling body, the blood literally spurting from her wrist. She felt the wire tighten as the Remington fell, then actually saw the severed hand still tight around the grip. But when Klein finally advanced, the blade sweeping down to the doctor's throat, Annie decided she had seen enough.

Her eyes were still shut when Klein cut the wire from her throat, released her wrists, and gathered her into his arms. But when at last he finally whispered her name, she couldn't help but look up into his eyes.

Tull had also begun to scream. Half crouched in the doorway of a smoldering barracks, spraying another full clip of flechettes into the wavering shadows, he was all the while screaming: "Well, come on in and get me! Come on!"

Slumped on the floor beside him, possibly still alive, was Wallace with a fist-sized hole in his left side and a fragment of steel still protruding from his thigh. The others, at least twenty-five former members of the Mojave security force, were clearly dead.

Tull jammed another clip into his M-90, squeezed off four more fast rounds, then pressed himself against the plaster and listened. Although there were still random shots from beyond the barracks, suddenly it was quiet. In fact, suddenly there were no sounds at all . . . except possibly a footstep or two.

Tull whirled, peering out into the swirling blackness. "Who's there?"

Then again, louder, because the first time he had only whispered it: "Who's out there?"

The voice that came, softly, calmly, could not have been more than a foot or two away.

"A friend of your father's," said Gray.

Tull seemed to nod, before he turned . . . a half nod of recognition, another whispered word: "Of course. I remember." But at the same time, he was also bringing the M-90 around, so that Gray couldn't wait any longer.

He fired from the hip, squeezing off four flechettes that lifted Tull into the air and slammed him against the plaster. Then, stepping forward for a last look at the man's face, he squeezed off another two rounds.

His mind, however, was entirely empty.

Epilogue

It was still dark when the Quick Response Unit finally descended on Mojave—first appearing out of the west, the TRU-ships and tactical assault crafts in black silhouette against the moonlight. It was also, of course, still very cold, but the sky was finally cloudless. Upon landing, they were met by some thirty surviving guards, who had gathered in a ragged line along the assembly yard.

As the first choppers drew lower, some shuffled forward, shielding their eyes against the blade-wash of dust. Most, however, simply continued watching the windows of those shattered barracks. Even when the first teams leapt from the doors, weapons locked and loaded, the guards remained silent. Nor did anyone respond when Strom appeared, demanding to know who was in charge.

It was nearly dawn before a semblance of order had been restored: photographs taken of the dead, clipped and monotone statements of survivors recorded, the bodies bagged, the shell fragments collected, a dozen or so pages of Wimple's notebook filled with tell-tale observations.

Through most of these proceedings, Wimple had remained alone . . . wandering among the debris, occasionally kicking at the charred remains of a body. Then finally closing his notebook, he lit a cigarette and sank to a rock in what had been Tull's cactus garden. Although still very cold, his raincoat was unfastened, his tie undone.

"You weren't surprised for a moment, were you?" said Strom from behind.

Wimple cocked his head to the side but otherwise remained unmoving: elbows resting on his knees, raincoat draped from his shoulders, eyes fixed on what had once been Tull's living quarters. "What makes you say that?"

"It was obvious."

"So?"

"So I think it's about time you talked to me."

Wimple shrugged, reached into the pocket of his raincoat, and withdrew the plastic casing from a spent flechette. "Recognize this?"

Strom took the casing from Wimple's open palm and held it to the light. Before she could offer an opinion, however, Wimple said, "Figueroa Armory."

Strom took another step forward and squatted to her haunches. In khakis and a safari hat, she looked vaguely like a character from a particularly tasteless cartoon series called *Combat Women*.

"Way I figure it," Wimple said, "is that they loaded the inmates on the buses and trucks some time last night. Some of them might have had to pile on top, but they eventually got them all."

"And went where?"

Wimple nodded to the ring of distant mountains only just now beginning to glow with the rising sun. "Out there," he said.

Strom glanced at her wristwatch. "Which means that at, say, fifty KPHs, it would place them somewhere in that first range."

Wimple nodded. "Probably."

"Which, in turn, means that if we scramble, we might be able to still catch them. They might still be in the foothills."

"Maybe."

Strom shifted her gaze to Wimple's profile: badly shaven, lips cracked from the wind. "Or maybe not?"

Wimple rose to his feet and slowly swept his arm across the far horizon. "You ever been out there?" he asked. "Goddamn wilderness. Caves. Ravines. Gorges. Hell, there's even still a couple of wolves out there. And a lot of places to hide, especially once they reach the timberline. And when you figure that they also got heat-seekers, frankly I wouldn't even risk it. Leastways not without some serious organization, which means at least a Tokyo authority."

"So what do you suggest?"

Wimple shrugged. "I'm a cop, Miss Strom. Not a soldier."

She also rose to her feet. "And what's that supposed to mean?"

He turned and looked at her; for the first time since they had left the city, he actually turned and locked into her gaze. "It means that this is no longer a police matter," he said. "It's a military matter. Because what you're facing out there is no longer a party of escaped inmates. What you're facing out there is an army, a full-blown revolutionary army. Now, at the moment they probably don't have a whole lot going for them in the way of equipment, but they're still an army, and the sooner you recognize that, the sooner you'll understand what these Whistlers are all about."

DAVID DRAKE

__NORTHWORLD__ 0-441-84830-3/$3.95

The consensus ruled twelve hundred worlds—but not Northworld.
Three fleets had been dispatched to probe the enigma of Northworld. None returned. Now, Commissioner Nils Hansen must
face the challenge of the distant planet. There he will confront a
world at war, a world of androids...all unique, all lethal.

__SURFACE ACTION__ 0-441-36375-X/$3.95

Venus has been transformed into a world of underwater habitats
for Earth's survivors. Battles on Venus must be fought on the
ocean's exotic surface. Johnnie Gordon trained his entire life for
battle, and now his time hås come to live a warrior's life on the
high seas.

THE FLEET Edited by David Drake and Bill Fawcett

The soldiers of the Human/Alien Alliance come from different
worlds and different cultures. But they share a common mission:
to reclaim occupied space from the savage Khalian invaders.

       __BREAKTHROUGH__   0-441-24105-0/$3.95
       __COUNTERATTACK__   0-441-24104-2/$3.95
       __SWORN ALLIES__   0-441-24090-9/$3.95

317